What if you went back in time to stop the September 11th terrorist attacks?

One man did.

This is his story.

Time is running out for Joshua Sinclair-he's stuck in the year 1987-with only one mission-warn the world of the events of September 11th, 2001-the only way to prevent his father's death at the Pentagon. But no one believes what he has to say. Even worse, a group of CIA officers are tracking his every move, trying to stop him at every possible turn. With no one in the past he can trust, Joshua must take fate into his own hands-from Chicago, Washington, and West Berlin...to the battlefields of Soviet-occupied Afghanistan.

From inside the novel...

"They must bring everything in from Kabul-fuel, water, rations. They're bleeding their treasuries pretending to be kings."

Joshua was distracted by a noise from the sky. An airplane approached. An Antonov cargo jet buzzed over their heads. Almost too close. But it was the color that burned into his mind.

The plane was painted orange. Neon pink and bright orange.

"What the hell?" muttered Joshua.

"We're going to have front row seats."

The plane circled around the valley and began its approach. It was a gigantic airplane. One of the Antonov models was the largest plane ever built to carry cargo and passengers. Joshua was terrible at identifying aircraft. The pilot flew the plane as if he was some sort of daredevil, swooping down after he had finished a full 360 around the base. Like he was landing in the Alaska bush. Except the plane had six jet engines.

Some kind of horn sounded from the hills below. Al-Zawairi passed him a pair of binoculars. "You might want these."

Joshua took them. Followed the plane as it landed and taxied in.

Then the air craft exploded.

Superstring Revolution

Shane O'Brien MacDonald

Ankerville Street Productions North America

First digital edition February 2015
ISBN: 978-0-9939323-4-2
First trade paperback edition February 2015
ISBN: 978-0-9939323-5-9

Found an error in one of our books?
Don't get angry, get us to fix it!
Contact us:
Ankerville Street Productions North America
ankervillestreetprods@gmail.com

Cover design by Yukiko Sato

Part One

The French-Swiss Border
Near Geneva

2017

1

In the beginning, there came the beeping sound. It was followed by a hum. The sound of power. Voltage. Waves of energy coursing through cabling. It had barely made a complete circuit when the fans kicked in. Great giant monsters of machinery. Originally built for an insane Chinese mining project at the base of a volcano. The sounds built upon one another. The heat rose, not quite oven temperature, but close. Engineers had spent months preparing for this day. Even a small miscalculation could overload the power grid of central Europe.

The announcer came over the headset frequency. "Start of experiment Hebert nine-one-one-two-five alpha. Mankind's first leap into teleportation technology. T minus ten...."

The sounds became monstrous.

2

The control room was enormous. It had been built for a future expansion that had yet to happen. One wall, easily a dozen meters tall, was nothing but visual displays. Multiple readouts bordering a large central viewscreen. Showing every important bit of data produced by the Large Hadron Collider.

Today, though, only a small crowd of scientists and technicians huddled around a bank of consoles. Each flashed a display with multiple colors and graphs, detailing the functions of the collider, providing feedback on what was happening a kilometer away from the control room. A cylinder shaped schematic displayed the cryogenic status of the mechanism. Too hot, and the entire thing would shut down. If the graph hit the red line, it was curtains for this experiment. Half the people in the room feared this would happen before they could stabilize the collision beam, their main tool used to observe how extraordinarily tiny bits of energy and matter interact.

Another chart showed the status of the computer grid, details of how fast the data connected to the control room. If it fused or shut down, they'd have no way of knowing what was going on. Next to it was the magnetic conduit status. They had to be perfectly aligned. If the beam was off by even a few gluons, failure was inevitable.

On a third screen came the energy consumed by the machine. The readout said 'Main Power throughput-56% and rising.' No one had ever dared push it to one hundred percent.

At the center of the bank of consoles sat two men with their fingers on the controls-Joshua Sinclair and François Hebert. Joshua looked at his monitor. "Magnetic confinement at ten to the minus ten."

François shook his head. "We need more power. That field has to be tighter."

Joshua stabbed at his console. "Throughput at sixty-eight percent. Confinement field at ten to the minus thirteen. Electron beam charge ramping up. Will reach full intensity in eighteen seconds."

"We need more power."

"The cryogens are approaching the blue line. Power at four hundred tee-ee-vee and rising."

"Fifteen seconds to beam flat top," came the announcer's voice.

Joshua shook his head. François was nuts to push the equipment this hard. The announcer was getting to his him. No wonder, with all the renovations they'd done. The whole set up looked like mission control at NASA. Some manager up in Geneva had the bright idea to add a countdown to the whole affair. Hire some guy from Florida, a real pro, watching the thing live, to announce it. Add a touch of drama to the occasion. These kind of experiments were falling out of the public consciousness. This was a way to put them back in.

Joshua looked back at the power readout. If it got too hot it would burn out the data cabling from the sensors. If that happened, they'd have nothing but junk from the experiment. "Magnetic confinement at ten to the minus eighteen and climbing. Throughput at ninety-one percent."

"Push it to one hundred."

Joshua's eyes almost bugged out. "Are you nuts? We're almost at the red line."

François glared at him. "Do it."

"Okay."

A phone rang. One of the Dutch scientists picked it up. "François," she yelled. "Axel's on the line. He says to dump the beam-"

"Tell him to fuck off."

"Magnetic confinement at ten to the minus fifty-four."

The announcer came on the speaker. "Beam power flat top in five...four...."

"To the minus twenty-two...."

"Three...."

"To the minus thirty-three...."

"Two...."

"Holy fuck...to the minus thirty-six."

"One...."

And at that moment in the control room, everything went just about apeshit.

3

The staff had named the chamber 'The Gulag.' When the beam was running the room was kept in a chilled vacuum. Once the air came in, the convection from the oxygen warmed everything up. It was the most important area, because it allowed the scientists to make visual and other observations as the electron beam hit an object.

Today that object was a Lego astronaut man.

He was positioned exactly in the path of the electron beam on a stand. In the center of his chest, the plastic had been carved out and replaced by a thin layer of beryllium.

In every other experiment, of which there are many every day, the electron beam is invisible. Not today. Out of nowhere a thin blue light shot out of the tunnel, into the large cavern of the gulag, going right through the beryllium.

Simultaneously on the chamber wall, a long black pipe vibrated. Slightly, then violently. It ripped lose from the latticework of metal supports, flying through an opening between struts. Revealing thick cables of blue, red and black.

The long black cable came loose from the wall, flying around like a fire hose spurting sparks.

4

Take a meter stick. Divide it into ten equal pieces. Throw nine of them away. Now you have a ten centimeter stick. This is ten to the minus one. Repeat the process. You get a centimeter-long piece of material-ten to the minus two. A millimeter is ten to the minus three. At ten to the minus five you get to the width of a red blood cell. Ten to the minus ten is the size of an atom. At ten to the minus thirty-five all possible measurements cease, at least according to accepted scientific dogma. Consider a width of human hair. Think about how wide that hair is compared to the known size of the observable universe. Now imagine if that single strand of hair was enlarged to appear the same size as the observable universe. Ten to the minus thirty-five would now be roughly the equivalent in size to a human hair. That's how small it is. Yet Joshua's readout gave him something at ten to the minus thirty-six. Seemingly impossible. Maybe an error. But the computer should be correcting for it.

Joshua's excitement was short lived as every screen in the control center started flashing. Every display showing power unit status went from green to red. Alarms sounded. Joshua glanced at the video feed from the gulag. He saw the black cable. The blue beam of electrons was something he'd never seen before.

Sparks from the cable flew into the beam. Everything went dark-the lights in the gulag, the controls, the lights in the control room. Only the video wall stayed operational. Everyone watched as the gulag filled with blue lightning. From a loudspeaker at a nearby station came the sound of an explosion.

The lights came back on.

François swiveled to Joshua. "Dump the beam."

Joshua leaned over and turned a big red dial. "Dumping." The collider was powering down.

François looked up at the viewscreen. "God... what did we do?"

Joshua was concerned with the cryogens, which had gone way past the red line. The collider had to be kept ultra cool, or it wouldn't operate properly. Some of the experiments scheduled for later that afternoon would no doubt be delayed. Some of the sensors weren't working. The data cable network was on the fritz. Something was broken. He looked up at the displays showing the power packs. Some had returned to green status, but most were still red.

François clicked on his display. "Radiation levels dropping rapidly."

It was only then that Joshua looked around and saw the entire staff staring up at the video feed from the gulag. He hadn't glanced at it. Smoke was drifting up from the bottom of the frame. In fact, you might have thought the room was on fire. The vacuum had been unsealed.

"What the hell happened?" he said. "Did we break it?"

5

Joshua met François when they were both working at Los Alamos, New Mexico. They started work the same week. François had arrived from the Perimeter Institute in Waterloo, Ontario. He was happy to be working in a town that wasn't in the snow belt. Joshua had come from the University of Chicago. He was glad to afford a house in a neighborhood where the person next door hadn't been gunned down by a cocaine dealer. And also happened to be in the snow belt.

Los Alamos had only one problem for two single men: it was devoid of young women who weren't married or attending the local high school. Los Alamos is a terrible sausage factory.

While the housing in New Mexico was cheaper, getting a cab to Santa Fe on the weekends could easily eat up much of a young scientist's savings.

That seemed to be their only opportunity for women, given that Los Alamos had more churches than drinking establishments. So François and Joshua would split the fare each weekend. One time, to save some money, they'd gone to a redneck bar a bit closer. Big mistake. One of the local cowboys took issue with François's French-Canadian accent and a fight ensued. Broken up by the local sheriff sitting two tables over, once he'd gotten his fill of these two city slickers getting their asses kicked.

They had both applied for funding from CERN, and as luck would have it, they moved over to Europe at the same time. Their collaboration was ongoing, despite several objections by the management. It seemed the two scientists weren't critical enough of each other's ideas.

Which was how they ended up here. Repairing computer cables. The gulag was a thirty-minute drive from the control room. Then a hundred meters underground. On the opposite side of the collider ring from the control center. And no one else was available for repairs on this particular day. Most of the personnel had their annual safety training seminar scheduled.

"All for a god damned data cable," said Joshua, looking down through the metal grid of the stairs. It was a long way to the bottom if they dropped something. They both carried metal briefcases, loaded up with a selection of cables and switches. As well as basic electrical tools.

François, being from Montreal, was always better dressed than Joshua, even when he was repairing a set of wires. He fit in well in Europe. Joshua dressed more like what he was-a post-graduate American scientist going from job to job, looking for the ever-elusive holy grail of academic tenure. So he could teach bored eighteen-year-olds basic calculus.

"I just don't understand how the air got in," said Joshua.

"The power grid fluctuated. The air conditioning that kept the vacuum in check must have failed. We were lucky the whole thing didn't go up like a barbecue."

"Yeah, I suppose. You can explain it to them. I mean, you did sell them this experiment like you were Neil Armstrong. Now people will think we're the gong show."

"If the magnet readings were correct-"

"Sure. But everything went haywire, so, who knows? I doubt we've found your spin foam today." Joshua stopped on the landing, putting down his briefcase. His arm was getting tired. "With all the billions put into this thing, you'd think they could install a few more elevators."

"They did," said François. "It's two kilometers back on your right."

"God, sending us down here. They must have other people."

"Yes, but Axel is pretty pissed about me not dumping the beam when he asked. He spent months overseeing the renovations last year, so he's on the hook if we burn out the new magnetic confinement system."

"He's not the happiest guy, is he?"

"No. That's what living in Geneva for twenty years will do to you. And then, I guess, today is a problem for him every year."

"Me too, I suppose."

François shook his head. "You've got a pretty cool head on your shoulders. And you don't enforce your grief on others."

Joshua wiped his brow. "Yeah." He looked up at the room. It was enormous. Enough to fill half a baseball stadium. Or a couple of cathedrals. The energy it must take to form a vacuum in here. They couldn't build the room any smaller and expect the level of heat dissipation from the cryonic systems. The whole place was a cavern of metal. So many different materials. In the bright lights you half-expected it to be the hive for some alien race of insects.

Joshua looked over at François, who had his smartphone out. "Did you download that app?"

"I did."

"And?"

Joshua bit his lip. It was the first application for a phone he'd ever made. This was his first sale, only yesterday.

François looked up at him. "I'm not a stockbroker."

"You don't need to be a stockbroker."

18

"Sure." François wasn't convinced. "Look, I'm just saying I'm not your target audience."

"But you plan to retire some day?"

"Yeah, but right now I have no money. Being a scientist and whatnot."

Joshua shook his head. But he understood François's dismay. The chances that he'd make money on it were pretty much nil. In his heart of hearts, he wished he could get into something a bit more lucrative than pure scientific research. It felt like most of the people using the facility these days were all tenured professors. They had a steady paycheck. For life. Not him. That was the fate of most young scientists these days.

François stood up. "Let's go. Only four hundred more steps."

Joshua sighed. They'd also have to climb those steps on their way back up.

6

"Look at this. The boron must have sparked on the accelerator stream."

Joshua and François had made it to the bottom of the gulag. François examined the charred cables. Surprised that something would have affected the data conduits.

"You'd think with all the energy pumping through here that power lines would be the problem," said Joshua, handing over a replacement wire.

François took out a portable jeweler's solder and attached the cable. "There, that's it. You could get a monkey to do this job."

Joshua took out a voltmeter and checked the connection. "Good to go. The redundant memory should be intact. I'm getting a current."

"Wonderful. All those fail safes we installed last year actually work."

François's radio beeped. He touched the earpiece. "Hello... What?" Surprise crawled across his face. "Okay. We're heading back up."

Joshua looked over at him with dismay. "What is it?"

"I don't want to spoil the surprise. Wait until we get back to the control center."

7

It had been a grueling drive returning to the control building for Joshua. François was remaining tight lipped, claiming he didn't want to make any sweeping statements until he'd seen the data. All the driving around was one thing Joshua hated about the job. With the new renovations to the collider, the younger scientists were asked to help with maintenance from time to time. Give them an appreciation for the toys they were playing with.

Someone had kindly brought a plate of sandwiches to one of the far corners of the room. While they snacked and sipped coffee, the two scientists looked at tablets of data that had been crunched by one of their colleagues. All within the last hour. The results...were spectacular. François had gone off and disappeared for a few minutes, only to return with a stack of paper.

Joshua shook his head. "You printed it off?"

"I had to see it with my own eyes. It's there. For real."

Joshua grabbed the pages from him. Skimmed them until he came to the part where the beam power had flat topped. He was astonished.

"And?" said François. "You see it, too, right? It's not just an error on the monitor?"

Joshua flipped through the pages again.

"This really isn't my specialty-"

"Is it right or isn't it?"

"It's there," he said.

"This is unbelievable! It could change the entire direction of mathematics."

Joshua smiled at the hyperbole. But François wasn't too far off in his excitement. There were various groups all throughout the world working on string theory. Some of them had come up with some pretty outrageous math. After today many of them would have to abandon their efforts.

Joshua's phone rang. "Hello? Yeah.... Okay.... Bye." He disconnected and looked over at François. A disconcerted look crossed his face. "That was Axel. He wants to see us."

8

During the renovations the previous year, Axel had arranged for a complete redo of the CERN office's interior design. After two months the functional white walls and Ikea furniture had been transformed into a neon wonderland. Gone were the hard angles of Northern European wood. Pink and bright green Formica in their place. Curves and polka dots. Half the walls in wild wallpaper murals of New York City or Tokyo. The furniture looked like it was hijacked from a Hong Kong modernist Italian furniture shop. Axel wasn't sure if he liked it. In ten or fifteen years an entire generation of scientists might be cursing these choices. To be fair, the office now looked like the makers of Frisbees had gone nuts.

Most of the scientists and support staff had their desks in the large, open-plan office that took up most of the floor. Along the edge of the north wall were the private offices of the senior scientists. Axel Straussbecker had occupied the only corner room for two years now. He was well used to his role as a manager, keeping things moving with grant applications and appeals to European politicians. In a couple of years he could contemplate retirement. He was long past the age where he did any real science. For men in his specialty, very little groundbreaking work was expected past the age of thirty.

From the edge of the office he saw Joshua and François approach. These two had really fucked up the experiment schedule. For the rest of the week, certainly. Possibly for the rest of the month.

François knocked at the door. Axel beckoned them in. "Sit down."

Once they were seated, François spoke first. "I'm really sorry about not taking your-"

"The collider will be shut down for twelve hours because you didn't take my call."

"I'll assume full responsibility. But considering the data we-"

"What about the other scientists? And the cost of bringing in specialized maintenance workers?"

François was ready for this. He leaned forward, sliding the printout in front of Axel. "Take a look. We might have discovered a new kind of physics today."

Axel's gaze didn't waver. "Bullshit. You're covering your arse. We both know it's probably a computational error."

"Sure, the schedule will be delayed. There's a buffer next week. We could use it to reconfirm the results."

"And let you burn this place to the ground? Absolutely not."

François threw his arms up in disgust. In one angry movement he stood up and stormed towards the door. "If only I'd been born white enough."

Joshua winced. Axel, dressed as sternly as a Hamburg banker, with a German accent that gave his words an icicle-like edge, often seemed like just another racist white European to François. People he'd seen far too often on the way up.

After François slammed the door on the way out, Joshua locked Axel in a death stare. "What the hell is wrong with you? Your medication ran out? Not enough time with your therapist?"

Axel sneered. "How dare you take that tone with me."

"Oh, please. My father died that day, too. But I do my job-"

"Go."

"We really don't need this kind of drama-"

"Go. Leave." Axel turned away.

Joshua sighed and walked out.

Axel watched him go. When he was well out of sight, Axel walked over to the glass wall that separated his office from the main area. Closed the curtains. And looked up at the clock above his door. 10:38 a.m. Well, he'd finished everything he'd planned to do today. He opened the cabinet from behind his desk. Grabbed a glass. From behind a wall of files he found a bottle of Jim Beam. As he poured himself a drink, his eyes cast on the digital calendar that told him it was September 11th, 2017.

9

Joshua didn't go back to the control room immediately. He left the main building and wandered the CERN campus. Walking in the bright September sunshine for at least fifteen minutes. He didn't want to face those monitors, those people. Not just yet. Axel's emotional state had really pissed him off.

When he got back to the control room, the entire staff had gathered in one spot, in front of the massive wall screen. Someone had turned on the CNN feed.

Joshua sauntered up to François. "What's going on?"

"I don't know. Looks like they caught one of the guys. The big one."

"Huh?"

"You know, in al-Qaeda."

"Why is this worthy of the big screen?"

"I guess this is like, the real guy," said François.

"You know how it is with the Americans. They're always looking for new people to arrest."

"Well," said Joshua, "this is a huge advancement. Usually they just blow these people away. With missiles or drones."

François turned away from the screen. "By the way, did I tell you? The BBC are coming here. This afternoon."

"To do what?"

"They're filming a documentary on me."

"Really?" Joshua smiled. "So you got pissed at Axel and called them?"

"No, no, they've been talking to me about this for weeks and weeks. They had a last minute rescheduling with a camera crew in Geneva."

Joshua looked up at the screen. The anchor was interviewing a man in an officer's uniform. The lower third said 'Retired General Jack MacLean.' He was a burly old bastard. Probably a total asshole, thought Joshua. He had a face like a cement cinderblock. All wrinkles and chin. Everything about him said 'America First.'

"It wasn't until last year," said General MacLean, "that we actually found this guy. Some of the intelligence was procured by our German...uh, partners. Who, I might add, are doing outstanding work. We're still waiting to hear from them on the whole chain of events."

"But is it true, General, that there's a Soviet connection here? Some have said that al-Zawahiri had connections to Russian intelligence."

"I don't know if that's true or not. But certainly his arrest is of extraordinary importance to the war on terror."

The CNN anchor held his cynical expression. Joshua noted the newscaster's slicked back hair and perfectly tailored suit. He didn't seem like the kind of guy who would have seen much action from a war zone. "But General, to be honest, we've had the arrest of no less than three masterminds after nine-eleven."

"Yes, but-"

"How are the American public to believe this is of such importance?"

"Well, you see, David-"

"And why would they care if proper judicial procedures aren't going to be undertaken? Most of these guys end up hidden away in Guantanamo Bay. The government has had few actual successes getting convictions for these people. Isn't that true?"

"Well, you have to understand this is a very difficult situation. There's a lot of fluidity in the judicial community."

The screen changed from General MacLean to police cars speeding through the streets of some Arab country, lights flashing. A title appeared indicating this was Peshawar. A grey-haired, bespectacled man came next. This must be Ayman al-Zawahiri, thought Joshua. He was led away in chains to a military vehicle. For extradition to the United States. "How convenient," said Joshua. "Ever since the American government started to pour tons of money into the new Pakistani regime. This must be payback for stopping all the drone strikes."

The images cut back to the anchor. "But can you comment on where you received this intelligence? To make the arrest?"

"Well, here we have," said MacLean, "an individual who's been on our radar for years. It's been difficult to gather a complete picture. However, today an enormous amount of information has been confiscated."

"Are you saying the original prosecution of the nine-eleven attacks was flawed? That they put away the wrong men?"

MacLean winced. "I don't want to say that. But it's possible the old case was an incomplete picture."

"How so?" asked the anchor.

François nudged Joshua as the General droned on. "One of your old CIA buddies?"

"I don't have 'buddies' from those days."

François was one of the few people at CERN that knew Joshua had gone to school on the GI bill. Most people in Europe probably didn't even know American veterans got free tuition. He'd done a tour in Afghanistan. As an enlisted soldier. Then someone who knew his father had recruited him for more sensitive assignments. Later he had worked at Langley. Even now, four of his family members worked in Washington. He was seen as a bit of a freak by them, choosing science over being a bureaucrat. Still, indirectly, and in some cases directly, he was paid by the government.

Joshua turned his attention back to the screen. "What's more," said MacLean, "is evidence that this al-Zawahiri had detailed plans for dozens, if not hundreds, of attacks on American soil. And our allies."

"General," said the anchor, "is this arrest more significant than the death of Osama bin Laden?"

"Symbolically, he was an important figure. But in practical terms, today is very significant."

"Perfect timing," said Joshua. "They've known this guy was the lynchpin since the mid-2000's. They just wanted to parade him out when the time was right."

"Everyone loves an anniversary," said François. "They'll ride this into the mid-term elections next year."

"You know Americans. We love voting."

At the console in front of Joshua the phone rang. "Hello?" he said. "Hey...yeah.... I'm watching it now...sure...tomorrow...okay. Bye." He hung up and turned to François. "It seems it's your lucky day, too. Axel had a change of heart."

"Really? Did he explain why?"

"Didn't say a damn thing. Count your lucky stars. You're on for tomorrow night."

10

Joshua found the one good thing about working at CERN was the borderline excellent food. A far cry from the Tex-Mex mediocrity served up by the surly staff at the Livermore Lab. In Europe he'd found they knew how to do food a lot better. Walking into the main cafeteria, he spotted a camera crew setting up around François. At the far end of the dining hall. He was getting his day in the sun.

The cafeteria, with its wide panoramic windows flushing in sunshine, had become the main interview spot for visiting journalists.

Joshua grabbed a tray and wandered through the counters of food. The salad bar was excellent. They usually had poached salmon and sushi. At the bakery counter was a selection of quiches, rotated daily. The kind of thing he'd never seen in New Mexico. The researchers were lucky, with the campus set in such a suburban, nearly rural setting.

There were almost no restaurants within walking distance.

After grabbing a plate of salad, he moved over to the coffee machines. Hit the americano button. He sat down and nibbled on his salad, watching the BBC crew set up. They had what looked like a big black rectangle screwed onto the top of a stand, the kind used for loudspeakers. One of the men opened the flaps on the front, and it turned out to be a giant light. With three or four fluorescent tubes. Then they set up a white translucent sheet behind François, probably to block the light. Once that was completed, they ran a tape measure from François's face to the lens of the camera. A journalist in a suit and tie sat down across the table. Interesting. Joshua had never been interviewed for television before. Maybe someday. When he dove into a big project of his own.

Joshua fingered through his pocket. Grabbed his telephone. Put on his headphones. Plugged in the AC adapter from his jacket pocket. His smartphone drained power faster than it should have. Rather than replace it with a new iPhone, he stubbornly clung to his aging model. It did everything perfectly. Software engineers had a nasty habit of fucking up perfectly usable programs. The downside was every couple of hours he had to recharge it, which meant he carried the power cord everywhere.

He scrolled through the movies he'd downloaded. People thought he was crazy. Paying to download movies onto his phone. It helped pass the time in the control room, while he waited for the collider beam to reset. Right now he had about a hundred or so films. He hadn't seen Back to the Future in a while. The beginning would pass the time during lunch.

Across the room, one of the cafeteria workers set down a bowl of two eggs in front of François. He thanked her in French. The woman said something the British crew didn't catch.

"Oh," said the reporter, "she's telling you which one is raw. Right?"

"Yes," said François. "So, what should I do with this?"

"You can just leave it on the table." The journalist had a crisp English accent. "Why don't we do the egg part first?" He turned to his director, standing by the camera. "Then we'll start the interview for real." He turned back to François. "Okay?"

"Fine by me." He took the eggs out of the bowl. "Have you got a clear shot?"

"Don't worry," said the reporter. "We'll get some cutaways when you're finished."

François took a deep breath. "Are we rolling?"

"Yes," said the cameraman.

"Okay." François had done this before, the time a Canadian crew had come to Los Alamos. He had learned the importance of pausing before he answered. "The best way to explain the theory is with these two eggs." He picked them both up and examined them, then looked towards the interviewer. "To the naked eye, both appear identical. But if we roll them on a flat surface-" He grabbed the eggs and spun them around like a top. One of them stayed perfectly in place. The other rolled away. François caught it before he fell to the floor. "So, now we know, even though they look the same, that the one spinning in place is hard-boiled. This demonstrates how humans perceive parallel universes. If we saw them from earth, they might look identical to ours. It is only by examining spacetime at a very small level that we can find out how all matter and energy in our universe spins. But when you break things down far enough, the different universes are interchangeable."

"Ah," said the reporter, "are you saying that the stars in our night sky could belong to a different universe?"

"Exactly," said François. "All with different laws of physics and chemistry, and god knows what else. It's possible, in the math we've developed, that our universe may be pushing on others. And given the gravitic distortions caused by black holes, they may be tearing at the fabric of our universe, allowing energy and light to leak out from others. Elements of spacetime that would normally be too large to leak through the interuniverse membrane. These other universes could be operating at a different speed of time than we are. We look up at the sky and assume it is part of our universe. But maybe it has actually poured through from other dimensions."

"Like a wrinkle in time?"

"More a rip, like in a bag of milk. Of course these rips are very, very small. We're viewing the cumulative effect. It's like steam leaking up through floorboards. You can't see the stove, but you know cooking is going on. My hope in the experiments we're doing is by opening a rip in the fabric of spacetime, it would create a shortcut through our universe. Hence, teleportation."

"But how would that happen?"

François smiled. "The math we've created indicates that when you get down far enough in spacetime, the material of our universe is quite porous. But only on the smallest possible level. We're trying to squeeze material so small that it actually falls through from one universe to another. Because, according to our mathematics, they all exist in the same place at the same time. It's only because the stuff we're made of has so much space between the particles that we don't fall through these gaps in spacetime, into other universes."

"But if we go back in time," said the reporter, "particles got denser and denser. Just like humans were apes, which were reptiles, from fish, all the way to bacteria."

"Yes, that's a reasonable way of putting it. We've discovered an error-code, just like that in computers, that arises from all the mathematical models. Some believe it's a kind of Darwinian mechanism, sifting out the less useful particles, and keeping those that make up spacetime in our universe. So what you see around you is just one layer of an infinite stack of universes."

François paused. "Is that clear?"

The reporter just smiled.

11

The camera crew switched off their lights just as Joshua finished his salad. In less than five minutes they had their equipment packed up. François shook all their hands, directing them out of the building. After grabbing a coffee, he sat down across from Joshua.

"Well, how was that?"

François shrugged. "They probably think I'm a kook. I don't think he was one of their regular guys. Usually they have someone who's a real scientist doing these things. He said he was investigating Red Cross funding in Syria. So I don't think he knew anything about what I was saying."

"Good for you. They'll have to put you on TV. He didn't ask the hard biting questions.

"Yeah, I suppose." François stirred a packet of sugar into his coffee. "The camera guy kept asking me where he could find a decent bar in

Geneva. I smiled and said, 'I don't know. It's Geneva. There are no good drinking establishments. Unless you like to hang out with bureaucrats from the World Health Organization.' It's not exactly London, is it?"

"Nah."

François pulled out his telephone. "So, this app you made. What am I supposed to do with it?"

"I thought you looked it over."

"I did. But I don't know how to use it. You didn't tell me what it's for."

"Look, here-" Joshua moved over next to him, taking the phone. "First, there's this button here-" He tapped the screen, loading a new menu. "It's a database of stock prices. You type in the stock or mutual fund you want, and the date. Then you get the historic price, its volatility, and movement. And its beta."

"What?"

"The beta. A measurement of risk."

"Sorry, I don't speak banker. But, look, I think you can do this on Yahoo for free. Can't you?"

"That database is in the cloud. This thing you can carry with you. On your phone. You don't need an internet connection. Let's say you're on a train, or in a car. You want to look up the price of Coca-cola stock for the last twenty-five years."

"So it's clogging up my hard drive?"

"No, it's revolutionary." Joshua swiped the screen over. "You can pick and match a bunch of companies. It'll do a historical regression. On all the equities. You set your investment period, then pick a bunch of stocks, and it'll give you an allocation. Or you can set the amount of money you want to make, and it will calculate how that grew in the past. To produce the results you wanted. Just set the date you want to buy, and the date you want to sell. It will give you a range of possibilities, and a probability that the results can be replicated again. Just like a weather report. You can also set the amount of risk you want to take on, and it will set the time period to buy and hold." He pressed a big green button. A new screen appeared with results. "And voila...an entire historic investment strategy."

"That's great," said François. "All you need to do is go back in time and rob a bank."

"Well, I'm hoping someone will buy it. Just to keep it off the market. Or make it into a proprietary software, like a Bloomberg terminal. Right now all these bankers are loaded with cash, but they don't know how to allocate it. And I'm sure every hedge fund trader that does active trading will want one of these."

"Why?"

"Because it has a lot of buttons. And it spits out numbers and graphs and pie charts. Look at the display. All the fancy colors and things that flash. I took time to consult a graphic designer. Make it fancy. Just like our monitors in the control room. It beeps when results appear. Active managers

43

can show it to clients. Pretend they're basing their choices on evidence."

"That's total nonsense. You can set any mathematical assumptions you want, and come up with exactly the desired results."

"Exactly."

Two of the women from their lab passed by, saying hi to François. He nodded and smiled. The girls giggled. Joshua watched them walk away. Both grad students who, unfortunately, were married.

François leaned over. "You want to go to Lyon this weekend to pick up girls?"

12

Lyon was practically a paradise compared to living in Geneva, thought Joshua. Sure, working at CERN was an honor. Playing with such expensive toys. Working with the brightest minds in physics and math. It was wonderful for the campus to feel cut off from everything. But it was also horrible.

It didn't help that Switzerland was so expensive. Filled with bureaucrats and foreign aid organizations, Geneva's women didn't seem all that interested in scientists doing theoretical research. Nor were the night club crowds particularly young there. Since François spoke French, and Joshua was attempting to learn it, they would hop in a car and drive to Lyon, just like they used to do in Santa Fe. It was about an hour and a half away. But everything in France was a third the price of Geneva. Joshua often bought his groceries on the French side of the border, anyway. His pay was good, but it wasn't that good.

It was the next day after the BBC interview. After dealing with all the problems with the collider, François would certainly want to take a vacation. They had spent hours trying to reduce the oscillations of the electron beam. Finally, after a full afternoon of dumping and restarting, they had stabilized things.

François paced anxiously. This was his only window to rerun the experiment. And the equipment didn't want to cooperate. A line of monitors on one of the consoles flashed red. Then an alarm sounded.

François threw his hands up in the air. The data connection went out again. "This was supposed to be fixed."

"It was," said Joshua. "There's no reason the sensors wouldn't be relaying data."

"The beam was up and running this morning. The computer grid was fine."

Joshua flicked through some menus. "Here's the problem. A cable must have shorted out again. It's knocked out the sensors in G sector. In the gulag."

François shook his head. "Someone has to go down there and replace it."

"Hey, wait a-"

"The maintenance people are all off tonight. We'll never get another chance this year with the way the schedule's booked."

"I don't know...it'll take me two hours to get there and back."

"You know how to fix it."

"So do you."

"I'd go down there, but someone has to keep an eye on things up here."

Joshua held up his fist. "On three." He counted down.

Joshua picked rock.

But François picked paper. "Now you can skip the gym tomorrow."

13

It was a long drive through the dark country roads. Joshua parked his car outside the service entrance to the gulag and headed on down. For some reason, his thoughts were fixated on his love life tonight. Or his lack thereof. He'd been at CERN for the last eight months. Most days he pulled twelve to eighteen hours at the site. Sure, it wasn't the sausage party Los Alamos was, but he knew he needed something more in his life. François had been dating some Swedish researcher that Joshua thought was butt-ugly, but at least she was blond. Maybe lowered expectations were the name of the game.

Oh, the life of a dedicated scientist.

He headed down the endless steel-grate steps. Three levels down he reached the airlock to the gulag. He called the control room on his radio. "Are the air conditioners set to open?"

"You're all set," came François's voice over the com link.

Joshua keyed in the pass code to the giant metal door. Heard the sealing mechanism hiss. The entrance slid open. God help anyone who got stuck down there when the vacuum pumps were on. They could clear the room of air in three minutes. And your lungs with it. The noise would drown out any kind of microphone. Not to mention the fact that sound doesn't travel in a vacuum.

He opened a storage locker and grabbed a tool kit. Picked a selection of cables. Last time, with two people, they'd been able to lug down a wide variety of tools. This time Joshua would just have to guess. He headed down the last four hundred steps.

At the bottom he looked up at the cathedral-like space. It was almost beautiful in its intricacy. Endless metal tubing and wiring. Grids of materials. Power cabling. He walked across the chamber. Took off some panels with a screwdriver. Checked the voltage. After twenty minutes of searching he found the problem. A cable had shorted. Again. Joshua got on his radio. "Found the faulty line. It's three meters away from the previous rupture. My fix will work for now, but we've got to get the engineers down here."

With all the current they were pumping into the collider, the designers had to be careful to make sure all the cabling was well isolated. Or the electricity would arc. This must be what was happening with the optical data network. Joshua took out a pair of pliers and a soldering gun and got to work. He dug up two bits of red wire from the wall panel that had sparked.

He turned around to reach for a smaller pair of pliers when his eye caught something else. A long black power cable. It had become detached from the opposite wall and had ripped off. An exposed end glowed red. The same situation as before. Joshua hit his microphone. "Uh, François, I think we have a bigger problem than the data cable."

"What's that?" came the crackly response.

Before Joshua could respond, everything went black.

14

In the control room a horrific hum was building. They had a direct audio feed on one of the video channels. All the panels flashed red. The collider beam had started up by itself. François examined the oscillations of the electrons on his monitor plot. His head flushed with fear and surprise. They only had five other people there tonight. Everyone else was off-shift.

François leaned into his microphone. "Uh...Joshua. I think you should get to an evac tube. Strange things are happening up here. The beam has just started up on its own, and we can't dump it."

"Why not?"

"I don't know. The computer's gone haywire."

"But I'd be able to hear something. Can you put the lights back on?"

In the gulag, Joshua looked around, his flashlight beam cutting through the darkness. Either way, he had to get out of here. Who knows what other problems could be caused by the loss of current?

Just as he started walking to the stairwell, a rumbling sound roared up the collider tunnel, like a freight train.

He had to go. Now.

Then things got fucking weird.

The air around him began to sparkle. The light flashed at a high frequency, like a strobe light. From the collider tunnel, blue lightening appeared. What was it? Some sort of static electricity? The last time Joshua had seen something like this was back in college, when someone had built a Tesla coil with beer bottles.

In the control room, François was watching the video feed. "Joshua, get out of there-" he yelled into the microphone. The audio had gone dead. Some sort of electromagnetic interference with the pickups and the RF transmitters. The optical data network was down, all the monitors flashing alerts for their lack of information.

"Joshua!"

In the collider, the ball of turquoise-blue lightening roared through the gulag. It reached Joshua and stopped, halting in mid-air. He expected a shock, but felt nothing as it enveloped his body. That made sense, the levels of power of an electronvolt were many times smaller than anything present in a human body. This cloud of...stuff...couldn't possibly injure him. Right?

The organic material in his body slowed the energy cloud down.

His hand. He could see through his hand. Joshua closed his eyes. He disappeared as the ball of lightning pushed through him, continuing on its way.

The lights came back on in the gulag.

Now empty.

Part Two

West Germany

1987

15

"He's the governor of Schleswig-Holstein," said MacLean.

The soldier sat behind a desk in an elaborate office on the top floor of a modern building overlooking the Rhine river in Bonn. Major Jack MacLean looked exactly the same as he would thirty years later on television, giving an interview about the capture of al-Zawahiri. But with fewer wrinkles around his eyes. And no grey hairs. In 1987, those things were still a ways off.

Sitting across from him was Raven Qaddumi. Definitively, he thought, one of the most attractive black women he'd ever seen. Of course, she wasn't completely black-her mother was a Palestinian who had settled in Washington. Still...MacLean put it out of his mind. He had to be all business with her. Now that he was on loan to the CIA.

MacLean had just handed the folder over to Raven. He had spent the morning reviewing it for this meeting. Uwe Berlioz, forty-seven years old. Born in Altenholz, a small town outside of Kiel, a city an hour's drive from the Danish border. Had spent time in Berlin, in the BND, the German security services. After that got a law degree from the University of Göttingen. Ran for the Landtag, the state parliament, when he was thirty-six. Became governor of Schleswig-Holstein, the state that stretches from Hamburg to the Danish border, at the age of forty-three. Earlier this year he'd been re-elected, although the campaign had been acrimonious, with accusations of fraud concerning land leasing agreements directed towards Berlioz's side. Many people thought he only got re-elected because he was good friends with the German chancellor Helmut Kohl.

Raven looked back down at the file folder. It was thick. "You expect this to be wrapped up in a month?"

"He's a very high profile candidate," said MacLean, his eyes darting around his lavishly appointed office.

Raven leaned back against her brocade chair. They sure as hell treated MacLean well. She couldn't get over the size of the office he had here. A huge oak desk. Walls adorned with swords and other memorabilia. And tapestries. She had also not failed to notice, next to the window, a well stocked liquor cabinet. It gave the impression that if MacLean was dealing with a file, it meant business. She looked at the photo of Uwe Berlioz. He was middle-aged, but still very handsome. She could see him locking up the female vote.

Raven looked over at MacLean. "This looks like it might get complicated."

"That's why we brought you in. Your work in Guinea-Bissau has been first rate. There's been a lot of discussion about you in Washington. No one ever expected anyone to make progress in some third world shithole like that. Although up here, the way we play things is a different ball game. You wouldn't have so much autonomy. So, in some ways, this assignment might not be as exciting for you."

A grin spread across Raven's face. Any place in Germany was better than Guinea-Bissau. Nineteen months earlier she had been stationed at the American diplomatic mission in Bissau, a city that was perhaps the poorest in West Africa, save for the capital of Equatorial Guinea. She had arrived with the recently-installed Communist government wrecking havoc on the local population, in the name of the world socialist revolution.

Within days of her arrival, Raven had met with various groups operating in the interior of the country. Most of them were little more than tribal leaders. However there was one man, Domingos Gomes, from a group called Bafata, who took a liking to her. She came back to visit him many times. They reached an agreement-the Americans would arrange shipments of arms, and in exchange, once a new government was in power, Bafata would promise to restore elections and promote democracy. Like many other poor countries, Guinea-Bissau had become a proxy war between America and the Soviet Union.

"My mission there certainly accomplished its goals and then some," said Raven. "But I like clean drinking water from my kitchen sink. Also, the communist regime is still in power down in Bissau, so I wouldn't say my mission is a total success."

"Nonsense," said MacLean. "You get things done. Better than those frat boys from Georgetown I usually deal with."

Raven smiled. "Well, at least I can put my German and Russian skills to use."

"Yes...." MacLean twisted one of his cufflinks. This was the part he found to be a bit of an unsavory request. "We want you to be seen with him."

"Excuse me?"

"I need to know if you have a boyfriend."

Raven looked at him, astonished. "Why? Are you expecting me to sleep with someone?"

"No," said MacLean. "But I need you to be seen with the gentleman in that dossier. I don't want to be asking this, but I need you to answer truthfully."

Raven's gaze narrowed. "No."

"No boyfriend?"

"None."

"And you're not married?"

"At the moment, no husband."

"No, uh...girlfriend."

Raven smiled.

"I have to ask this," said MacLean, "I'm sorry."

"No, no one at all." Raven looked down at the folder on her lap. "Are you expecting me to take my clothing off?"

"Of course not. But we may need you to kiss. But no, uh, tongue. It's just to get some compromising photos. Something to make his wife upset."

"That sounds immoral." Raven seriously didn't like the idea of this.

"We don't want to send them to her, just have them on file. In case Herr Berlioz gets out of line. Give our side some advantage if we need to negotiate."

"I see."

"The CIA wants this guy to disappear, but we need to know more about him before we make a move. So we were hoping you could befriend him. Maybe even leak a bit of bait to get him hooked."

"Such as?"

"Signals intelligence that is useless to us but might be of interest to a local German politician. Things like, say, the people who've been smuggling diamonds and tractor parts across the Danish border. Or the members of his Bundesland security service also on the payroll of the East German government. These local krauts eat that kind of stuff up."

Raven stood up, even though the meeting wasn't over. "And when I'm done here, you're going to send me back to West Africa?"

"Well, if that's what you wanted-"

"Absolutely not."

"Then," said MacLean, "if you do this for me, I'll pull every string to get you put back in Washington, if it's what you want."

"It is."

"Of course, I can't promise anything. Showing competence in Africa usually means you'll be transferred to Sweden or Finland. At least, that's my reading of the bureaucratic mentality."

Raven nodded. She knew the score. Her life was far from unusual for those working overseas under the State Department. She herself was from a family of civil servants, but Raven was the first to work for State.

With that, MacLean handed her an envelope containing a plane ticket. "We've arranged for a hotel room in Hamburg. There you will liaise with the British."

"Really? Why are we bringing them in on this?"

"As a favor. They have some logistical advantages in Germany we can make use of."

Raven nodded. They made some more small talk about life in West Germany, then Raven left and went back to her hotel in Cologne. She didn't want to stay in Bonn. Too small, too boring. And filled with government bureaucrats. It was like a mini-Geneva. Not her kind of place. But Cologne, only twenty minutes away, was a completely different story.

She wished she had more time to visit. Despite being close to Bonn, Cologne was a lot more fun. People had a reputation for partying it up. Taking too many holidays, as one of her German colleagues had once told her. Certainly a far cry from the small town that served as the capital if the Federal Republic of Germany. Even Hamburg, with all the vibrancy of being a port city, couldn't compare.

The next day, she left by plane. It was a short sixty-minute flight to Hamburg. After collecting her luggage, Raven took the shuttle bus to a hotel across the street from the Hamburg Hauptbanhof, the main train station. According to the file, tomorrow she would be met by Henderson, a man from British intelligence. Most of the way from the airport she slept. Waking just in time for the bus to pull into the front driveway of the hotel.

The driver grabbed her small suitcase, passing it to her as the rain drizzled down. She smiled, thanked him in German, and entered the lobby. Grand and ornate, she was the only black woman there. As expected. Shouldn't be too hard for her to be spotted. One thing was certain, she wouldn't be asked to do any foot surveillance work here. Not with the way she blended in.

"Ms. Qaddumi?" came a voice with a thick Northern English accent.

Raven turned around. A thin, balding man with a ring of short-cropped hair appeared next to her, wearing a navy double-breasted suit. He could have been a chauffeur, if only he had the right hat.

"Yes?" she said.

"Please follow me."

"And you are?"

"A friend of Mr. MacLean."

"I'd like to ditch my luggage, first."

The man looked surprised, as if this wasn't part of the script he'd memorized. "Yes, of course. I'll await your return."

In her room Raven made a quick call to MacLean. "Probably the Brits going ahead of schedule," he said. "They want to help us out."

"Great. Well, you know where to send my remains."

"Ha, ha," said MacLean. "I doubt you're popular enough to warrant a hit squad."

She returned to the lobby and followed the man out to an Alfa Romero executive car. He walked around to the driver's side. Raven decided to sit in the front.

The vehicle was comfortable, but it hardly glided over the road like a Cadillac. They pulled into a line of what looked like brick warehouses along the Elbe river. Cars were already lined up in front of them.

"I don't see a ferry dock," said Raven.

"We're taking the elevator. In case someone wants to tail us." This was the first thing the guy had said during the entire drive.

They waited in line twenty minuets until they pulled into a wooden elevator that was big enough to fit, at most, three or four cars. Down they went, the doors opening on a single-lane tunnel. On the other side they drove onto an identical car elevator.

Pulling out, they emerged in a warehouse district. Surrounded by factories and shipping concerns. The drizzle coated the landscape with a dull grey. The driver took a bunch of turns before they arrived at an ancient brick warehouse.

"Follow me upstairs," said her driver.

They climbed all the way up to the fourth floor. Knocking three times, the driver and Raven were led into a narrow hallway by a bearded middle-aged man. After closing the door, he extended his hand to Raven. "Ms. Qaddumi, it is a pleasure to meet you. My name is Robert Henderson."

Raven smiled, looking down the dark, narrow corridor. "You don't believe in turning on the lights?" She shook his hand.

"Less for someone to see through an open door. Follow me."

Henderson led her down a series of corridors. At one point the driver disappeared. They emerged into a large open space. Cardboard boxes loaded with gift wrapping paper stood stacked five meters high, surrounding the edge of the room. In the center were desks and tables, some piled with files, others with different kinds of electronic equipment. On a far wall a map was posted next to a board of surveillance photographs. A lone secretary smiled at them as they passed the bank of desks.

"Officially, our business is paper products. A German sales distributor for a Canadian firm."

"And unofficially?"

"West German branch of MI6." Henderson led her to a kitchen in the rear. A meeting table took up most of the space. "Please have a seat. Can I offer you a cup of coffee?"

"That would be great."

Raven walked around to the head of the table, where someone had left a manila folder. Her name was stenciled on the top.

"Those are our field guidelines. Of course, we intend to help the CIA in any way possible. Just that we want to make sure we're all operating on the same page."

"Certainly," she said, sitting down and opening the folder. While Henderson brewed a fresh pot of coffee, she read through the manuals.

Once brewed, Henderson left a coffee on the table for her and disappeared for half an hour. When he returned, Raven was on the last page of the dossier.

"You people don't seem too enthusiastic to be helping us," she said.

"London is completely ambivalent," said

Henderson. "But personally, I don't mind. Whitehall is always cutting our budget. Helping out the CIA just means one more favor to pull in later on."

"Well, I'm glad to hear that."

"Now that the formalities are out of the way, let me take you to the apartment. We've set you up in a place near the Reeperbahn."

"On the main street?"

"No, we didn't think you'd be...that kind of girl. But not too far away."

Raven smiled. The Reeperbahn was the street that housed Hamburg's red light district. The sleaze intermingled with family-friendly entertainment and high-end restaurants. Something that most Americans found shocking.

The apartment was in a small brick building, across from a parking lot used by cement trucks. Far from glamorous. Indeed, it seemed to be more of a converted loft than a place to live. She imagined the other units would be ideal for artists, and told Henderson so.

"Yes," he said. "Photographers, too. Lots of people coming and going. No one notices us carrying around strange lenses or microphones."

Raven looked around the place. The large living area was shared with a kitchen. Ornate double doors opened onto a spacious bedroom. The front wall had sixteen-foot windows, reaching up to the ceiling. They looked out over the truck lot across the street. Over the entrance to the lot was a small construction trailer.

Henderson pointed out the window. "You've got no neighbors over there. Our man will be in the trailer with a camera. So you can pull the curtains at your pleasure. But if they're open, we have a full view of the whole flat, except the toilet at the rear."

"Quite the find."

"Indeed. We got lucky. Your CIA associates would kill for a place like this."

16

Raven's dress was Chanel, and glittered in the headlights of the hired car. Despite the resources of the American government, the State Department foreign missions were kept to a strict budget. They didn't have an extra vehicle to spare. Ordinarily Raven would be concerned about bugging devices, but for this kind of mission, being bugged actually furthered her aims.

The parameters of her assignment were simple: get Uwe Berlioz back to the loft. And get him to kiss her in front of the cameras. After that, the mission was...as they euphemistically put it...at her discretion.

She had been given an invite for a reception put on by the Norwegian consulate. It was the kind of event that wavered between low-key and deadly dull. So that Uwe Berlioz, as someone from a neighboring German Bundesland drumming up business for the local factories, wouldn't have much at stake.

The event was held in a small ballroom of the Ritz Hotel. A beautiful old building which had survived the war, and had a balcony overlooking the Alster. A far more glamorous location than such an event called for. That was probably why the room was packed. The Norwegians had put out some real money to get this location.

Raven joined a group with one of the American consular delegates she had worked with in Washington, until a conversation about German nuclear policy became too much for her. She moved around the ballroom. At the drinks table she was chatted up by a Swedish delegate. He was elderly, and charming. A man from a Götenberg family that owned a logging concern. After a pleasant five minute chat, she spotted Berlioz at the drinks table. He was alone. She said goodbye to the logging baron and moved in for the kill.

Raven leaned over the table and grabbed a glass of wine, bumping Berlioz's arm. "Oh, I'm so clumsy."

Uwe turned around. "Not unlike American foreign policy."

"Well you're one to talk-" Raven wanted to slap the guy, but immediately was taken with his smile. He was tall, and looked good in a suit. His voice stirred something in her she hadn't felt in a long time.

"Of course, I should apologize. You Americans are thin skinned."

Raven turned around, half out of offense, half out of nervousness. She headed for the balcony to get some air. In no way had she expected him to be so...attractive.

Outside the rain had stopped. She looked out over the railing towards the Alster. At night Hamburg could be a quiet town, couldn't it? Thoughts raced through her mind. Could she really deceive this guy? The whole mission was making her uncomfortable.

Raven took out one of her cigarettes. It was then she saw Uwe approach.

"Can I light it for you?"

"You're too kind," she said.

"Not at all. Most of the women I meet from America are already married."

Raven looked away. "I was married. Years ago."

"The foreign service life was too much for him?"

"Something like that," she said. "What about you? You don't seem like the bachelor type."

Uwe sighed. "I'm not."

"Your wife is here?"

"No, it's a long complicated story." Uwe looked in at the ballroom. "I don't really want to go back in there. I've talked to enough Scandinavian industrialists tonight."

"Me too."

"Do you live in Hamburg?"

"Yes."

"I know a great restaurant near here."

"I don't know...."

"Well, if you prefer the company of lumber barons...." Uwe walked away, leaving her alone on the balcony.

Three hours later, some of the crowd had thinned out. Raven caught sight of Uwe smoking alone on the balcony, and joined him.

"How are you holding up?" she asked. "I saw you shaking a lot of hands."

"Yes, one of the hazards of the job. He reached over and lit her cigarette. Tell me, are you living near the American consulate?"

"No, actually, my apartment is in St. Pauli."

"In the Reeperbahn?"

Raven giggled. "Not exactly. But close."

"Fantastic. That restaurant I told you about is right nearby." He took her hand, but she retracted it. Uwe moved in closer to her. "Look, any minute now, one of my party colleagues will be out here dragging me to another bar to debate economic policy. We'd better go now, or you might never see me again." He turned around and walked away.

Raven followed him.

A short cab ride later and they were at the Royal Napoleon, a Belgian restaurant. The maitre d' knew Uwe well. Raven surprised him by ordering off the German menu.

"I'm shocked," said Uwe after the waiter had returned to the kitchen. "I thought most Americans only spoke English."

"I'm not most Americans," she said. They made more small talk about bars in Washington. It seemed Uwe had a keen interest in America. Their food arrived and Raven thought it was delicious, especially since it was the first real meal she'd eaten all day.

By the time the bill came, they were on their third glass of wine. "So tell me," said Raven, "you know so much about the States. Why?"

Uwe swigged the rest of his glass. "The honest to god truth is that I'd love to live some place like America. Where summers aren't always cloudy and grey. Lots of land around your house."

"I grew up in the D.C. area, so we've got problems all our own."

"Yes, all the crime. Am I right?"

"Yeah. Washington has been having a rough decade. I enjoy living in Germany. For the most part it's safe. Even if my looks get a few stares here and there. The Hamburg consulate sure is better than Bonn."

Uwe laughed. "They put the capital there for the day Germany is reunited. So no one will complain when they move it back to Berlin."

"You think we'll see that in our lifetime?"

"Of course. The Russian bear will have to go into hibernation some time, right?"

"Is that what Chancellor Kohl says?"

"That's what I say."

"Really?"

Uwe smiled. "It is."

"You seem very well connected, politically."

"Of course."

"I had no idea the head of the Bundesland were... so important."

"Yes, yes. We are like your state governors in America. Perhaps more so. Germans are very parochial. Those of us in the north tend to cast a wary eye on the southerners."

"Really?"

"Sometimes I can barely understand what they are saying. Many there speak a very strange dialect form of German." Uwe grabbed the bill.

"No, you don't have to-"

He waved her away. As they left the restaurant, Raven began to giggle.

"What is it?" asked Uwe.

"This is so embarrassing," said Raven.

"What?"

"I have no idea how to get back to my apartment."

"Do you have the address?"

Raven produced a piece of paper.

Uwe looked at it. "Oh, that's not too far."

"How will you get home?"

"If you can call me a cab...."

"Of course."

"Here," he said, "we have to turn this way."

He led her onto a darkened side street. They got about fifty feet from the main road when Raven spotted four men, all in black leather jackets and with shaved heads. One of them began shouting. Raven took a moment to figure out what they were saying, but it seemed to be something less than complimentary about black women being accompanied by white men.

Uwe stopped and grabbed her arm. "Wait a moment." He walked over to the group while they were still in the middle of the road. Uwe screamed at them, while the tallest of the thugs raised a fist and took a swing at him.

Uwe screamed at the lead skinhead, who pushed him back. Despite it being a five-on-one match, Uwe twisted around and landed a blow to the guy's stomach, collapsing him to the ground, winded. But the guy behind moved towards Uwe, fists at the ready.

Raven ran up to them, then she heard one of the skinheads behind the lead guy scream Uwe's name.

The head guy in leather backed off when he heard the name Berlioz. His eyes widened. It was clear he was making the connection. He yelled at the group. They took off running.

"Oh, my god," said Raven, "you're bleeding."

"I'll be fine. They just winded me."

"You're not okay. Come with me." She dragged him back to the main street. To the restaurant they'd left only moments before.

Raven begged the maitre d' for a telephone. She called a taxi to pick them up. Their waiter arrived concerned, asking what had happened as he brought Uwe a cloth napkin to stop his bleeding head. Raven remained silent. She knew if she said anything, the restaurant staff would be the first to snitch to one of the newspapers. The driver said he was just around the corner.

Five minutes later they pulled up at Raven's apartment. It was a long climb up four flights of narrow stairs. She wished the Brits had gotten her some place with an elevator.

In the bathroom Uwe caught sight of the dried blood on his face. "Not bad, huh? I hope you will respect my street fighter politics now."

Raven found a first aid kit in one of the kitchen drawers. Taking out the peroxide and cotton swabs, she cleaned the cut on his chin. So much blood from such a small wound.

"You be careful, now," he said. "There are many others like them who don't like foreign people."

"It's okay. I'm sure Hamburg isn't usually that bad."

"No. You're right. I should go to the hospital, just in case it needs stitches."

"Are you sure you should be moving?"

"I'm okay, I don't want to trouble you." Uwe moved to the phone and called a taxi. Raven passed the piece of paper with her address on it to him. He took it, and had barely put down the receiver when the horn of a cab sounded outside.

"Thank you, you've been too kind," he said, moving for the door.

"It was nothing-" she said, but he was already gone. She looked out the window to the street below and saw him get into the taxi and drive off.

17

"Did you like the little show we put on? It wasn't easy finding thugs who would attack such a prominent man. They were terrified he would be surrounded by security."

Five minutes earlier Raven's slumber had been interrupted by a phone call from Henderson. Even though it was ten-thirty, she still felt the lingering effects of last night's wine.

"I hope those guys were okay," she said. "Uwe seems like quite the brawler." The skinhead thugs that had heckled them the previous evening had been hired by MI6.

For lunch she headed to a small market around the corner and bought bread, cold cuts and vegetables. She was cooking some red peppers when her doorbell rang. She buzzed the visitor in, expecting a British secret agent.

Instead it was a bouquet of flowers.

With a note from Uwe: "Call me at the office, I want to see you again." The message ended with the phone number of his secretary in Kiel. Raven smiled. He had taken the bait. Just to make sure she could reel Uwe in, she'd wait another day to get back to him.

Promptly at one o'clock, Henderson and his team arrived. They had rented the apartment above the one Raven occupied, as well as the one next door. They drilled a hole in the wall to the adjacent apartment, fitting a space wide enough for three camera lenses.

"Isn't one enough?" she asked.

"More is better," said Henderson. "One stays on the wide, another up above to get a bird's eye view, and one in the middle to zoom in. We'll cover it up with a floor to ceiling mirror."

"And the bedroom...?"

"Is off limits to our devices. Feel free to strip down to your heart's delight."

Henderson moved into the kitchen. "Oh, I've interrupted you making lunch."

"Um, well...."

"I know a place a couple blocks away. We'll put it on my account, on behalf of all the inconvenience we're causing."

Thirty-five minutes later Raven sat across from Henderson in a Turkish restaurant on a wide boulevard, just north of the Reeperbahn. The coffee she had ordered was delicious.

"Something bothers you," said Henderson.

"Yes. It seems like a lot of equipment. I thought you just wanted photos of him kissing me."

Henderson put down his coffee, surprised. "MacLean didn't tell you?"

"What?"

"This has become a major operation. Ever since the election."

"What happened?"

Henderson looked around. "It's really not my place to say. But I'll tell you this-two foreign governments are operating out of Schleswig-Holstein."

"Doing what?"

"Military things."

"And?"

"They aren't exactly allies."

"I don't understand."

"Let's just say, not everyone believes in the spirit of international cooperation. Especially the people back home."

"You're talking in riddles," said Raven.

"I know. Putting it bluntly, you're in the thick of it, so don't get sloppy."

The next morning, Raven called the number on the card Uwe had given her. She felt nervous as she listened to the dial tone ring. What if he got suspicious? Would a woman calling him be too direct? What if he was too busy to take her call?

A woman's voice answered. Raven gave her name and asked for Uwe in German. And was surprised when she was immediately put through.

"I was thinking about you all night," he said.

"Really? Doing what?"

"You don't want to know."

"I do," she said. "What does a German politician do at work?"

"He thinks about strange American girls in Hamburg."

"What makes you think I'm strange?"

"I don't know. Maybe if I could see you again, I'd change my mind."

"Tonight? Are you busy?"

"Not at all."

At eight-thirty she heard the bell ring, and buzzed him in. The sound of scampering came from the apartment above. The true test of a secret agent, she thought. Pretending you weren't being watched.

A minute later came a knock on her door. Raven opened it, and there was the governor of Schleswig-Holstein, alone, carrying a bottle of wine and two large Styrofoam containers.

"I hope you enjoy Turkish food," he said.

"Of course," she said. I'd better, she thought, after having it two days in a row.

Uwe walked over to the large windows looking out over the street. The first thing he did was close the curtains.

This went uncommented by Raven. The man was worried. About what? Did he expect his wife to pass by?

As they ate Uwe told her all about Schleswig-Holstein. All the problems with smugglers, since it was so close to Scandinavia. "And those are just the criminals," he said. "Then there are all the Danes who come in just to buy cheaper alcohol."

Raven smiled.

He lit a cigarette. Raven walked over and brushed aside the curtains, opening the window.

"Won't it get cold in here?"

"Why?" she said, taking out a pack of Marlborough Menthols, "are you susceptible to pneumonia?"

"No, it's just-"

"You're worried someone will see you here?"

Uwe grimaced.

"Who?" asked Raven. "Your wife?"

"Yes," he said, pouring himself another cup of wine. "It's complicated. She was very stressed because of the election. Didn't like having to explain the situation to the children."

"How old are they?"

"Six and ten."

"So, old enough to read the papers?"

"For the boy, yes."

"Are they living in Hamburg?"

"No," he said, stubbing out his cigarette. "The children study at a boarding school near Frankfurt. We have a house in the west of Hamburg, but my wife has chosen to stay at her parent's home in Geneva for the last few months."

"She's Swiss?"

"Yes."

"And she's gone back to live with...."

"I think she may want to divorce me." Uwe took a sip of wine. "All the scandals. In the papers. And then I'm away all the time. Never in one place. She doesn't want to move to Kiel. Too far from shopping, I guess. So I only stay there a few nights a week."

"I know how you feel," said Raven. "About the whole traveling for the government thing. My ex-husband is back in Washington."

"You didn't get along?"

"He was...jealous of my success. If that's what you want to call it."

Uwe smiled. "You shouldn't be so modest."

"I've spent the last two years at the embassy in Guinea-Bissau. Not exactly the cream of the posting crop."

"What was it like?"

"It's a very poor country. Our compound at least had power most of the time. But the place is run by a communist dictatorship. So there's not a lot you can do. I wished there was some way I could have changed things there."

"I suppose," said Uwe, taking another bite of pita bread. "But change involves war. And once you commit yourself to that, things get messy pretty quickly." He took a sip of wine. "I would like to visit Guinea some time. I've heard the islands off the coast are beautiful."

Uwe stood up, and moved to the window. Surveying the street below, he seemed satisfied no one was watching him.

"Who are you looking for?" said Raven, moving over to sit on her leather sofa. "The press?"

"No," he said, moving over to sit down next to her. "I guess I feel a bit guilty."

"About what?"

Uwe gazed into her eyes. "May I be honest with you?"

"Of course."

"I've been thinking about you a lot the past few days. Ever since meeting on that balcony." He reached over and took her hand.

Raven didn't resist. In fact, looking at him now, she couldn't deny within herself a longing to be with him. What only she knew, and had confessed to no one, was that she hadn't been with a man in three years. Uwe had awakened a quiet desperation in her. She pulled closer to him, unable, and unwilling, to resist his body.

Unbeknownst to Uwe, an MI6 photographer was across the road, recording all the action with a telephoto lens. At first he got what he expected, shots of them making out. Perhaps the photographer had expected curtains to close, or something, but he got the shock of his life when he saw the couple get undressed on the couch and begin to make love. Hastily he reloaded his camera, capturing some intimate details before the couple scampered naked, to the loft's bedroom, shutting off the lights. For a moment, the British photographer felt a bit sleazy-this was the kind of thing the Russians tended to specialize in, not Her Majesty's civil servants.

Still, this was an American operation. He dialed Henderson's line at the Hamburg office, but got no answer, as expected. So he decided it was best to try the contact in Bonn. None of the MI6 boys wanted to deal with this anyway-their immediate reaction might be to burn the film. Carefully the photographer dialed the direct line to the CIA office in Plittersdorf.

MacLean sounded drunk when he answered the phone. "Look, I'm not here to tell you how to wipe your ass. Just get it done."

"So I should continue?" asked the photographer.

"She should have known to expect this. It's not my business to get involved with who she wants to fuck."

The photographer sighed. "Can you please just give me a clear set of instructions?"

Back in Bonn, MacLean looked around his office. He'd spent the last two hours looking through reports from signals intelligence. One hour ago he'd started on a bottle of Jim Beam. Holding a half-full glass in his hand, MacLean thought about it. If Raven was to get involved, this might be more valuable than just a set of cheeky photographs. She could pick the guy's brain. Put them in a proactive situation.

He cleared his throat. "Fine, pack your things up and go home for the night. Let them have their privacy."

18

Three months later, Uwe was having a rough time in the press. Raven had gone to Washington at the end of August to visit her family while the schools were still on vacation. She met the woman her husband had remarried. Like Raven, she also worked for the government, in Maryland. Everything was cordial, even if Raven felt like a fifth wheel some of the time. She saw her daughter, who was about to start school. Raven didn't discuss her feelings towards her children with anyone.

When she landed in Hamburg she bought a newspaper after seeing Uwe's name on the front page. There had been plenty of accusations of financial impropriety during his last Bundesland election campaign the previous spring. It was the reason his wife was never around. Instead of having her face dragged through the muck with Uwe, the wife, whose name was Hannah, had, it seemed, now permanently decamped to Geneva. Far from the eyes of the German press.

With his wife away, Raven began to fill the romantic void in Uwe's life. They still saw each other secretly. Each week Raven wrote a three page report for MacLean detailing everything she observed about Uwe and the workings of the Schleswig-Holstein government. But now, after months of pretending to like Uwe, she really felt she was falling in love with him.

The reports were beginning to make her feel like a traitor.

So it wasn't much of a surprise when, three days after returning from Washington, MacLean had summoned her to Bonn.

"Look," he said as Raven walked in the door, "you've got to do better than this. In the beginning we were getting some good stuff from this guy. But I send this to Washington and all they do is complain."

"Has it occurred to you that maybe there's nothing here of interest? Maybe this guy doesn't know very much."

MacLean shook his head. "Every single German state has its own spy bureau. If an agent of a foreign government so much as farts in the wrong direction they write a report about it. Who do you think runs this country? It ain't the good guys-it's the Nazis who got away with it after the war. Who have to keep tabs on the population. To make sure no one starts yelling to the press about who did what. If we put away every one who committed an atrocity, we'd have to lock up most of the wartime German army."

"Gee, thanks for the history lesson, professor." Raven sat down in front of the desk without asking permission. "I don't know what you expect me to do. It's not easy playing both sides. And frankly, it's not my field of expertise, either."

"Well, then make it your field."

"You put me in this position. Were you expecting me to do this forever? Frankly, if this is your idea of what a government employee is supposed to do, maybe you could find someone else. Down on the Reeperbahn, maybe."

"Are you saying you want to quit?"

"Maybe."

MacLean turned around, facing his window overlooking the Rhine. "It would be fair to say that we didn't plan for you to fall in love with him."

"Excuse me-"

"Why else would you consider quitting? Unless you wanted to stay here with him? You know the obvious move would be to transfer you somewhere else. But you don't want to go."

Raven stood up and walked over to the window. Below some children were kicking a soccer ball along the road. Probably Americans. Heading home after classes at the nearby embassy school. "It might help if you could tell me what this is all about. Why are we so interested in a third-tier European politician?"

"Because," said MacLean, "he has the ear of the West German Chancellor. They're good friends. And also he's the governor of the state that borders Denmark. So he has control over a vital link in all the shipping containers bound for the port at Copenhagen."

"And?"

"The real issue," said MacLean, "is all the arms flowing through Europe. From Israel."

"For who?"

"Iran."

"You must be joking. They're on opposite sides."

A grin spread across MacLean's face. "We're talking about the Middle East here. It's like a ball of yarn, the way these assholes are all intertwined. The right wingers in the Israeli Mossad like the idea of sending weapons to Iran, just to stir up the shit. But it looks bad if they went directly from the port at Haifa. So instead they're running them through Italy, all the way up north. In cargo containers labeled machine parts. At Copenhagen they're put on a ship bound for Iran. But the Danish have signaled frustrations with the Israelis, so there is talk of loading the ships from Kiel."

"Literally within sight of Uwe's office."

MacLean was taken aback by Raven's use of the governor's first name. "Berlioz? Yes. It's his turf. And many of us think the right wingers in the Mossad had something to do with all those nasty campaign allegations. So he would naturally be a thorn in the side of the operation. All of this is petty stuff. But these people are serious guys."

Raven shifted uncomfortably. "What do you want me to do?"

"Keep up business as usual. Just be aware of what you're in the middle of. It does me no favors to see you get hurt."

Raven looked over at him. It was the first time she'd seen a glimmer of sympathy in MacLean's tough exterior.

After that they switched to more mundane topics. Raven was getting a pay raise, compensation for the lack of an opening in Washington. Ten minutes later, MacLean was buzzed from the outer office. His next appointment arrived, and it was time for Raven to go back to Hamburg. The staff had called her a taxi.

Raven closed her eyes as the cab sped to the airport. It took a few minutes before she began to feel something was wrong. Rubbing her eyes, she looked out the window.

This wasn't the way to the airport-they'd passed the turn off and were heading into Cologne. Raven leaned forward. "Excuse me, I was going to the-"

The driver mumbled something into his radio, then handed the microphone to her.

The speaker on the handset crackled. "Excuse me, Ms. Qaddumi," said a voice in English layered with a thick German accent, "please relax. You and I are going to have a little talk. I will keep it brief, so you need not worry about missing your flight. The driver has only been hired for the day, and only speaks German. Please do not trouble yourself by jumping out of the cab."

Raven pressed the button on the side of the mike. "Who are you?"

"My name is Mendel. I freelance for various government agencies. Now get off the radio, and be patient."

She sat back, half alarmed, half curious. Who would go to such trouble? They had to have been staking out the embassy all afternoon. The phone lines were obviously compromised. But this Mendel fellow must have wanted her to know that. Some sort of carrot, to entice her to talk? He must assume that the NSA would want to sweep the lines for bugs now.

They pulled off the expressway and into Kalk, an uninspiring suburb east of downtown Cologne. Drove past rows of identical white apartment buildings to end up at a warehouse somewhere by the train tracks. A man in a shiny red raincoat stood on a loading dock. If this Mendel guy was a spy, she thought, he wasn't too good at sneaking around.

The driver beckoned her towards the man in the raincoat. Raven got out and walked towards him. "Why did you bring me here? Are you planning to kidnap me?"

The man smiled. "Pleased to meet you."

"What do you want? Are you working for the Russians?"

"Sometimes I do," he said, "but not today."

"Could you not have kept things simple and made an appointment?"

"I would have preferred to. But let's say things are far more complicated than you think, Ms. Qaddumi. It's best if I try to work in the shadows."

"Uh-huh."

"You, it seems, do not like to work covertly. And your presence here is complicating matters."

"How?"

"I'm not allowed to say-"

"So who do you work for?"

Mendel stared at her, unhappy to be interrupted. "For the Iranians. They've got a good thing going here. And they don't want you to fuck it up."

"Why would I do that?"

"Because," he said, "you're an idealist."

"Stop playing games."

"You are dating a man named Uwe Berlioz. It might be good if you looked into his dealings and tried to convince him to change his mind."

Raven was confused. Obviously this Mendel fellow thought she knew more than she actually did. She decided to play along. "I can't control what he wants to do. It's not my place to give him orders."

"Your life will be a lot longer if you dumped him."

"Is that a threat?"

Mendel moved in closer. "No, it's a wise piece of advice. You're sticking your toes into a nasty bath.

Your politician friend will need to cover his ass. And he'll throw you into a sea of bullets if he thinks it will save his skin."

"What are you saying? Is Uwe's life in danger?"

Mendel remained silent.

A car door opened behind Raven. The driver yelled at her that it was time to go to the airport.

"Good day, Ms. Qaddumi."

Later that day, when she got back to Hamburg, the first thing Raven did was call Uwe.

"I'm busy tonight," he said. "There is a charity ball in Kiel I have to attend."

"Cut out early and come over. I need to talk to you."

"What is so urgent?"

"Not on the phone. Tell me you'll come over later?"

"Fine."

Late that night, around 11:30, Uwe appeared at her door, drunk.

She took his hand and dragged him in. No words were exchanged before they got each other's clothes off. They made love furiously-it had been a couple of weeks since they'd been together. When it was all over, they lay in the bed, smoking.

"I heard your life is in danger," she said.

Uwe looked over and kissed her cheek. "You just found this out? I've known that for years. I'm sure half the men in my security service are East German double agents. If they wanted to get rid of me, they would have done so by now."

Uwe put out his cigarette and reached over for a glass of wine Raven had poured for him. "Some days I just want to be done with all of this."

"And do what?"

"Move to the Caribbean. Open an ice cream stand. Or a bar. With exotic dancers."

"I suppose you could do both. Make more money."

Uwe put his head in his hands. "Maybe I could emigrate to America. Put this life behind me."

Raven didn't respond. Uwe seemed to be serious about this.

"But first," he said, "things need to be taken care of. I'd have to divorce my wife."

19

Hannah Berlioz was not a woman who liked to make a scene. Perhaps that was why she and Uwe complimented each other so well for so long. She could be his rock, standing in the background, anchoring him from drifting away with some of his crazier ideas.

At least, until the election earlier this spring.

For years she had put up with the usual tirade of unfounded rumors that were typical in West German politics. Secret children. An unacknowledged wife across the border with the east. A heroin habit. All of it nonsense spread by his opponent. But when rumors of financial fraud-some sort of complicated bank transaction, that involved money for highway development funds and secret payments to Uwe's accounts in Switzerland-Hannah knew something felt different.

For one, these rumors were reported in the newspaper.

Despite this, she had stayed with Uwe all throughout the campaign. But afterwards, when she confronted him about the allegations, he was evasive. Saying something about how he wouldn't be in politics forever. That some things are more important than just pandering to voters.

And with that, she decided to move back to Geneva. She made the excuse that the public eye was too much for her. The stress was too much. So she went back to live with her mother in a suburb near the French border. Uwe didn't protest. He may love her, but she was still a lower priority than his work. With the children off to boarding school near Frankfurt, she told him she would be back when the school vacation started. They could at least behave themselves while the children were around. Uwe didn't protest her leaving. He was probably happy to have one less complication in his life, or so Hannah thought.

But now, she had checked their joint checking account and discovered that Uwe had yet to put in funds for the spring semester. Private school was expensive in Germany. And this particular school, in the suburbs of Frankfurt, charged exorbitant fees for late payments.

Hannah had flown in to Hamburg on an early morning flight. Catching a taxi at the airport, she didn't arrive at her and Uwe's house until mid-morning, which was fine. No chance she would be forced to talk to him. When they next spoke, he would probably be exhausted, giving her an advantage.

Their house was to the west of the city, in an affluent suburb along the Elbe river. It was one of two residences-the other was a country house in Schleswig-Holstein, where they spent a lot of time, mostly out of necessity given that the Hamburg house was in a different Bundesland.

The cab pulled up the side road that led to the front yard. The house had been built in the late 19th century, so it was considered fairly new in German terms. It looked like a near-replica of the White House in Washington, complete with colonial-style pillars on the front porch.

Hannah thought it gaudy-it was Uwe's decision to buy it. Wim Wenders had used it as a location in his film "The American Friend." This led to Uwe insisting they had to have it, despite already owning the house in the country. Hannah only went along with it because it was convenient for when she went shopping in the city.

The Turkish cab driver was kind enough to help her with the luggage to the front door. Once inside she surveyed the surroundings. The cleaning woman was still coming twice a week. She went upstairs to find the bedroom a mess. It looked like Uwe was coming back here tonight.

After tidying up the clothes strewn on the floor and making the bed, Hannah surveyed the rest of the rooms. While she ostensibly was just making sure the maid was dusting properly, her survey had the additional point of letting her know if anyone else had been staying at the house. But she could find no evidence of this. The place clearly had been inhabited by a single male.

In the kitchen she found the carcass of a take-out chicken in the fridge, and a supply of pasta dinners in the freezer. Along with other kinds of foods that microwaved easily. Also Uwe had well upped the supply and variety of beer in the kitchen. Hannah couldn't help but smile. She hated beer.

The survey of the house complete, her luggage had to be dealt with. As she unpacked, Hannah began to feel a bit of sympathy for Uwe. She had stayed with him through his hour of need, then he had treated her coldly. She swore she wasn't going to forgive him, but picking up his abandoned clothing off the floor dulled this pledge.

After making herself a sandwich, she decided to call his office.

The secretary answered, then kept her on hold. When the woman came back on the line, she told Hannah that Uwe would be home for dinner. Hannah shook her head when she hung up the phone.

The rest of the morning was spent cleaning up the house, then she drove into town to buy groceries. As the sun set, she busied about preparing hasenpfeffer, a rabbit stew that Uwe liked. Hannah had learned a decent recipe from her mother that was difficult to find in Northern German restaurants.

Around seven o'clock, she saw Uwe's car pull up. It was about an hour and a half drive from Kiel, where the Landtag for Schleswig-Holstein was located. He must have left early to come and see her. He rarely stayed in Hamburg during the work week.

Hannah was setting the table when he walked in.

"So you've come back," said Uwe.

"Yes. The children's tuition has to be paid."

"You came back because you want money."

Hannah rolled her eyes. "If that was all I wanted I would have divorced you."

They stared at each other for a long moment. Then Uwe approached and took her hand in his.

"The dinner is getting cold-" she said.

Uwe ignored her and started to take off her clothes. He knew they had the house to themselves. She giggled as he kissed her.

While they began to make love, using the dining room table in lieu of a bed, neither Uwe nor Hannah could have known about the man with the telephoto lens taking their picture from a duck blind he'd erected three nights before. The man, a Brit working with MI6, had taken much effort to avoid being seen.

The agent had snuck through the woods in the early morning hours. Found a position with a clear view of the house. Then built a tent and dug a latrine. He had lugged a bladder with eight liters of water, which, if he was careful, combined with the MREs he packed, would be enough to last five days, after which the team would reconsider the value of having him there. The man wasn't happy to have been given this task, but the overtime he was billing almost made up for his discomfort. He would make a month's worth of wages in less than a week.

Now, after all the boredom, he couldn't believe what he was seeing. The couple disrobed and made love right in front of the window. With the lights on. He switched on the shotgun microphone, and captured every grunt and moan. He took a couple of pictures, enough to confirm his story. When they were finished a few moments later, he recorded them pledging their love for each other.

This was major. Hannah and Uwe in love wasn't part of the narrative he'd been told. He'd best get in contact with the Americans.

The MI6 agent knew that things would get a lot more difficult from now on. He had been tasked to set up the post because his superiors were convinced the German politician would be taking girls back to his house. But that wasn't the case. They'd have to follow him in the city, with cars and foot patrols. To no certain conclusion. Or at least one thing was certain-it would cost the pursuers a lot of money. Tailing people, especially high profile individuals, easily racked up a small fortune in man hours in a short amount of time.

Knowing this, and the experience he had with intelligence bureaucracies, the MI6 agent guessed shortcuts would be taken. Sloppy shortcuts.

20

By the next evening the photos taken from the surveillance of Uwe's house had been developed. They had been couriered to Bonn, straight to MacLean's office. Unfortunately, they didn't arrive until after all of the staff had left. The courier had been left with clear instructions that someone would be there to sign for them, and he was not to leave until he had handed them over in person. Unlikely as it may seem, the person with MI6 in London who usually would send such a message had called in sick that day, and the replacement, a secretary from the Home Office, had been overwhelmed by an emergency cable from the British Embassy in Sri Lanka. So the CIA wasn't cabled. No one expected the package to arrive.

The courier, after much discussion with the front desk security guard, was escorted up to the CIA offices. Then spent five full minutes banging on the door until MacLean answered. He was the only person left in the darkened office.

Hearing the noise, he walked toward the locked entrance. He'd only left his office to go to the restroom. MacLean was drunk. While going through a stack of field reports, he'd also gone through a third of a bottle of Jim Beam.

At the door he took the package from the courier, and signed for it. Back in his office, he opened the file.

And was shocked by what he saw.

Not so much by the explicitness-MacLean was more amused by Uwe and his wife getting it off on the dining room table-it was more his anger from realizing the best laid plans could be foiled. Months of Raven's efforts would go down the drain. Sure, they hadn't learned anything incredibly useful, but this guy could still be a valuable source of info. Through Uwe they'd confirmed their picture of contraband arms smuggling through Europe. All the way to the port in Copenhagen. Stuff the Israelis weren't telling them, despite the Americans being their ally.

He had to calm down. MacLean put the photos aside. Kept drinking and going through the reports already on his desk.

When he was done with the documents that needed his attention, he put them in the office safe. But after filing them in the proper spot, he moved over to the photo cabinet on the other side of the closet-sized vault. Grabbed the file on Uwe.

Took out the photos of the governor making love with Raven. Most were blurry and out of focus, but it was clear what was going on. They showed him walking into her apartment, kissing, disrobing...and more stuff.

They always kept three sets of prints in a file coded with such high importance. MacLean grabbed one set and locked the safe for the night. Back at his office, despite his drunken stupor, he found a plain manila envelope. Copied Uwe's address from the photos that had just arrived that night, and placed the Raven photos inside. He was so drunk he didn't notice one of them fall to the floor, lodging itself halfway under his desk.

Then he placed a stamp on the letter, and put the envelope on top of the outgoing mail. The only thing he didn't do was write the CIA's return address on the correspondence. No amount of Jim Beam could make him do that.

The next morning, MacLean arrived at work at half past nine. He walked back to his office, and found the photo of Uwe and Raven in flagrante face down on the floor, partially obscured by his desk. This photo had to go back in the safe. He struggled to remember why he'd taken it out.

As he walked to the vault, the front office secretary smiled at him. "Oh, I got your letter," she said.

MacLean froze. "What letter?"

"The one you sent after the mail went out last night. You left it in the outgoing tray. I called them, and they were kind enough to send a truck around. As a special favor."

"What do you mean?"

"The large brown envelope. Sent to Hamburg."

"Where in Hamburg?"

The secretary thought hard. "I don't know. The neighborhood wasn't one of the central ones." She took out a slip of paper from her desk. "Oh, here it is." She checked a directory of postal codes. "That's in the west, by the river, I think."

Panic flooded MacLean's body. He bolted from the office and ran down to the building's mail room in the basement. The clerk there assured him the mail had already gone out.

The man led MacLean around a corner and out to the alley. Turning onto the street, about two hundred feet away, was a Deutsche Post delivery truck. Heading to the central post office. MacLean ran around to the parking garage and hopped in his Chrysler LeBaron. He caught up to the truck. The State Department building must be its last pick up of the morning-a negotiated favor, no doubt. For the next forty-five minutes, they played cat and mouse through the streets of Bonn, into the southern suburbs of Cologne. The truck finally stopped at a large postal sorting warehouse in the middle of an industrial estate.

MacLean got out and ran up to the driver. "You've got to help me, I'm looking for a letter."

The postal worker shouted a few words at him in

German, none of them pleasant sounding. MacLean switched to his limited vocabulary in the language. The German smiled. "Wait a moment," he said in English.

The man went inside, reappearing a couple of minutes later with an elderly gentleman, who must be a supervisor. The man asked what the trouble was in broken English.

But in the two minutes he'd been left alone to think about the situation, MacLean realized he'd probably made a mistake chasing down the mail.

Only State Department material was sent through the regular postal service. The CIA used a private courier, that forwarded the mail on to Frankfurt Airport.

MacLean apologized and made an excuse that someone had misinformed him about a package. Then he got in his car and left, leaving two very confused postal employees.

Back at the office, MacLean started work on a transfer for Raven. To get her back to Washington. It was the only thing he could do to cover his ass.

21

MacLean's letter arrived the next day in the late morning. Hannah was at home when the mail came. She was surprised to see the large envelope among the piles of bills and supermarket flyers. While the tabloid-size format was familiar to most Americans, Hannah had never seen something so large in the mail before. She immediately noticed it was labeled for Uwe, but had no return address. The post mark said Frankfurt. Could it be from the children's boarding school? Maybe they had been in a rush and forgotten to stamp it with their crest.

Her curiosity piqued, she left the mail on the side table by the door, except for the oversized envelope, which she brought with her into the kitchen where she had been preparing a pot roast. Sitting down at the table, she opened the letter.

The dozen or so black and white photos fell out, scattering in front of her. One of them had flipped over.

There they were. Raven and Uwe. Fucking.

She wanted to rip the image to shreds. Instead she walked over to the sink and began to cry.

After she had bawled for ten minutes, she shut off the pot roast and spent the rest of the day in bed. With a bottle of Riesling. She was all alone here for the next few days. No one would see her misery. That night she thought about phoning one of her friends in Geneva. Maybe she would go back there. How could she possibly put up with this?

She kept drinking all through the afternoon.

Eventually she made her way to the medicine cabinet. Found a bottle of benzodiazepines that she sometimes used to calm herself. The doctor had prescribed them for Uwe, but he hadn't used them in months.

The label said to only take one every twelve hours. But as the evening drew closer, she moved on to schnapps then back to white wine. Drinking while lying in the bed. She no longer cared for anything.

Hannah decided to take the rest of the pills. All at once.

But she was so drunk by that point that she only got halfway through the bottle before passing out. Her stomach, with almost no food in it, wasn't handling the sudden binge of alcohol all that well. Before the pills could take effect she woke, vomiting all over the white goose-down comforter.

112

The next day she woke up, still alive. And deeply ashamed of herself. She saw the half-empty pill bottle. This would have to be explained to Uwe. Her eyes glanced over the vomit-covered sheets. Disgusting. The rest of the day would be spent cleaning everything. And being miserable.

Two days later the bed still stank. The mattress would have to be replaced.

Meanwhile, Hannah's unhappiness had turned to anger. She had tried to rationalize Uwe's behavior. It wasn't the fact he cheated on her that made her angry...but that he had taken up with...a black woman. A foreigner. How could he do that? Choose such a woman over Hannah, with her perfect blond hair?

Examining the photos was painful. And useless. She'd never be able to find the woman, not from the angle the pictures were shot. It was not until she turned them over to put them back in the envelope that she saw the writing.

A filing number.

Time and date.

And most importantly, an address. Whoever had sent these didn't bother to make a duplicate. They'd just ripped them out of a filing cabinet, hadn't they?

Later that morning, Hannah went into the city. At a hardware store she bought locksmith tools. In college she had worked a part time job as a receptionist at a security firm. One of the employees, trying to impress her, had showed her how to get through most doors with a few simple items.

After that, she went to St. Pauli and found Raven's apartment easily. Hannah trudged all the way up to the forth floor. Made it through the door easily.

The apartment had been made to look like it was cheap, but Hannah knew the area well. Whoever owned this place had money. The whole thing seemed like a ruse. Or a movie set. How had Uwe not seen this? Something was very wrong with all of it.

She went to the closet. Found some of Uwe's clothing. So he was staying here? Living a secret life?

The asshole.

She ripped all of his things out and fled. Never once did she suspect the MI6 agent upstairs videotaping the whole thing.

22

The next night, Uwe came home. With a smile and hop to his step. He had barely entered the living room when he saw the clothing on the couch. His heart sank.

"So," said Hannah, appearing on the other side of the room, "it was too much to ask your girlfriend to come all the way out here?"

"Look," he said, "you know that I love you. It wasn't my intention to hurt you. But things are complicated-"

"How? It seems simple to me. You plan to screw any girl you want. Even some negress from blackest Africa-"

"Hey! Stop right there. She's American." Uwe started to gather up his clothes. "You were away. And I had no idea if you were ever coming back."

"This is how you treat me after standing by your side? Through that campaign? After having to listen to all the horrible rumors they made up? I stayed quiet. Made sure everything was there for you." She took a sip from a glass of wine in her hand. "We can't go on like this. What were you expecting, Uwe? That you'd run from me to your mistress and no one would ever notice? To carry on with the two of us at the same time in the same city? Me on the weekends and her during the week?"

Uwe sat down on the sofa, his body exhausted listening to her very astute logic. She was right. "Look...I'm sorry. You were away. I couldn't help myself. If it's what you want, I'll break it off. You are more valuable to me than anyone else. And for the sake of the children-"

"Really? Is that really true? Or are you just saying this because you don't want me to take the house from you? While you go and live with your girlfriend?"

"No," he said, "it's over. I'm tired of all the sneaking around."

Hannah shook her head and stomped off to the kitchen.

Uwe moved into the hallway. "I have to go back to work. I only came by to have dinner. When you've calmed down we can talk about this some more."

That night Uwe drove all the way back to the Landtag in Kiel. And buried himself in work. Went through all the files waiting for his attention on his desk. The truth was that he hadn't planned to come back, but it was better than sharing a house with an angry Hannah. Something, during the long stretch of autobahn into Kiel, had become clear to him. His career was going nowhere. He grabbed a file. More requisition forms from the Bundesland secret police. More need to hire people. To watch all the guns being run through Schleswig-Holstein. It was getting worse now that the Danes were upset with the Israelis. Another matter for the politicians to worry about. Another scandal on simmer for the time being. Maybe a second chance for the inept foreign policy of the German Federal Republic to drag his family through the mud. It was getting to be too much.

The next morning, after spending the night at his country house just outside Kiel, Uwe called a meeting of the head of the state police special forces. Two gentlemen arrived at his office at ten-thirty: the man with the crooked nose, Dreisler, and his assistant.

Uwe began. "You should know something."

"What's that?" said Dreisler.

"There are people who helped put me in power. People who have been very generous with money. Who I've helped liaise between their business interests and the port here in Kiel." Uwe leaned forward. "You and I both know about these shipments."

Dreisler smiled. "Of course."

"Well, we've got to shut this thing down. I will be resigning in the coming days."

The eyes of both men across the desk bulged out.

"But before I do that," said Uwe without missing a beat, "I've asked Chancellor Kohl for permission to testify at his committee for government corruption. The public one. In front of the television cameras. I want this all aired out in the open. Which will happen in two week's time. You should be well aware of the implications of this for your departments. I will not name any of you as accomplices. I will say, with all honesty, that we did not know about this for a long period of time."

"That's half-truth at best," said Dreisler.

"Sure, but it will keep us covered. But, as for the people running this pipeline of armaments, it could well blow up in their faces. And make a big scandal."

After Uwe dismissed the two men, Dreisler went back to his private office and dialed a number. The conversation would lead him to go down to the port later that night, and stand by a cargo container, waiting for Mendel.

The man with the crooked nose was a double-agent, also on the payrolls of the Stasi, the East German secret police. As a courtesy, this meeting with Mendel had been arranged. Even though Mendel was more-or-less a freelancer, he could take action that the man with the crooked nose couldn't. Still, it was important to avoid links between the two.

Dreisler didn't have to wait long. At half past eight, Mendel arrived in a blue Lada. After listening to Dreisler speak, he nodded. "I see. So Uwe Berlioz is going to give everything to the papers. So they can boost their circulation. That's what you're telling me?"

"Yes," said Dreisler.

"Well, it seems to me we have no choice. He's got to go. We'll have to bring in our friends from Tel Aviv."

"I understand," said Dreisler, "that you might want to do that, but please think about the idea of soft pressure. He has a family."

"So what?" said Mendel.

"And the Americans have one of their people tied up with him."

Mendel smiled. "Yes. I know about her. But the stupid Colonel running things down in Bonn sent some photos to Berlioz's wife. It's a big mess. There's no way he'll respond to the usual threats." Mendel shook his head, signaling a sense of resignation. "We'll have to talk to our friends in the Holy Land. But I'll see what I can do on my own first. Maybe he can be brought around."

Later that same night Uwe called Hannah and told her he was too busy to come back. But in fact, it was a lie-he'd actually gone to Raven's apartment in St. Pauli. They made love and drank wine.

"I don't want to break up with you," he said. Saying this despite knowing his loyalties were divided.

Raven nuzzled his chest hair. "Are you in love with me?"

Uwe smiled. "What kind of girl wants to spend their life with a middle-aged German politician?"

Raven looked over at him. "Are you sure you know me that well?"

Uwe nodded.

"Are you going to go back to your wife?"

"I don't know. I love both of you. It's a very complicated situation."

"It is," she said. "And I'm not sure I want to quit the State Department. And we both have families spread out all over...."

"You could take up residence in Germany. I could make that happen."

Raven smiled. "Why don't we go on vacation. Somewhere tropical. Away from the gloom. We can go together. And think about what we want to do."

Uwe took her hand. "That sounds like a good idea. It will give me some time to think."

"I'll get some time off."

The next day Uwe met Hannah back at the white house. It had been a couple of days since they'd seen each other. She had managed to calm down. Uwe found her in the kitchen, sipping wine.

"I want to quit," he said. "I want to do what's right. Go out with guns blazing. We have enough money saved up. Maybe I can go back to being a lawyer. See if I can find some contract work." He poured himself a glass of wine. "Take out the corrupt ones who have made a business running guns through Germany."

"What do you mean?" said Hannah.

"Expose these for who they are. It's a long, complicated story. And it's best you didn't know." He took a swig of Riesling. "All of it will come out in the papers. It will be a tough time."

"If it's what you want, I'll have to support you, won't I?" said Hannah.

Uwe put down his glass. "But first I want to take a vacation by myself. Think about what I want to say. I was hoping you could use that time to talk to the children. Almost certainly I'll come under public attack. My reputation will be shredded. And you should know you may come under scrutiny as well."

Hannah shook her head. "What is all this about?"

"I don't want to say. But it's international. And could lead to a massive upheaval of the global order. Or maybe it will result in nothing."

Later he phoned the travel agency, booking two tickets for himself and Raven. As he waited for the saleswoman to confirm his flight, Uwe thought about all the people he wanted to expose. Some of these people had put him in power. They wouldn't take his betrayal lightly. Nor would anyone ever be willing to trust him again. But it was still best for him to explain what he knew.

Just to make sure his story would make the papers in English, he phoned a reporter he knew from the International Herald Tribune. Left a message with the reporter's assistant with the details of the hotel he'd be staying at in St. Barts. Maybe not all of it would be publishable, but it would be scandalous nonetheless.

Uwe had no idea there were two MI6 agents in a van on the other side of the forest that surrounded his house, recording the entire conversation. MacLean would be well interested in hearing this.

23

After his re-election, Uwe had completely gutted his office of all the awards and medals he displayed on his desk and nearby shelves. As well as pictures hanging on the walls of Uwe with famous politicians and celebrities. He had wanted to give a more contrite impression to visitors. Today it finally hit him how austere the place was. Hopefully it made people think he took his job seriously. A politician who didn't believe in waste. Especially after all the accusations of graft that had been hurled at him. He'd even had the office manager change the chairs to designs that were far less comfortable. The only thing you could argue smacked of luxury was the office's view of the Danish Straits, connecting the Baltic with the North Sea. Not something that could be avoided.

This morning Uwe had already had a meeting with the Schleswig-Holstein planning commission, who were looking at a ludicrous idea to build a second Kiel canal to accommodate modern cruise ships. Uwe had been polite in his dismissals. The kind of tedious, useless meeting that one could never have imagined before becoming a politician. An hour into the discussion, Uwe began to zone out. He was grateful when his secretary came in and opened the door, signaling to the five bureaucrats that it was time to leave.

Then, precisely at eleven o'clock, John Steinberg arrived. The British lawyer had come all the way from Berlin, the city he currently made his base. He was one of the Christian Democrat's leading liaisons with the English speaking world. A man crucial when matters of trade and commerce arose. So of course Uwe had agreed to see him on less than twenty-four hour's notice.

But personally, Uwe was just happy that someone who was Jewish still lived in Germany. Not an easy decision, given the country's recent past.

"How are you?" said Uwe in welcoming English.

"Oh, very good, very good," said Steinberg.

"How are things in Berlin?"

"Oh, the usual. We're getting by. So busy all the time." Steinberg sat down.

"So what can I do for you today?"

"Well, there's an issue concerning your police force."

"Isn't their always?"

"Yes, well, they're very zealous."

Uwe leaned towards his intercom. "Can I offer you a cup of tea or some coffee?"

"Oh, no, I'm fine. There's no need for me to stay that long. I have other meetings in Hamburg later today. Have to get on the road soon. I was just asking if you could consider doing us a favor."

"'Us'?"

"Well, you see, there are these container lorries heading from Hamburg."

The emotion drained from Uwe's voice. "If you're referring to the shipments that were heading to Copenhagen, I've heard of them."

Steinberg looked uncomfortable, like he didn't want to be asking about this, but the matter was a necessary part of his job. "Schleswig-Holstein is a valuable transit route for many of my clients. Much of the cargo from Southern Europe runs through here."

"I see."

"Because of some difficulties with the Danish authorities, much more might be dispatched from the port of Kiel. I was hoping you could expedite matters. Try to avoid holding up our shipments."

Uwe grinned. "Business matters are always a priority of this government. There's no need to provide extra scrutiny. Unless your clients were doing something illegal."

"No, of course not," said Steinberg, almost embarrassed. "It's just the last couple months some businesses have worried about overzealous inspections. Perhaps in a need to put a public face on eradicating corruption. But slowing down transport routes wrecks quite a bit of havoc, you see. Even if the intentions are pure. I mean, nothing has ever been found."

"Of course not," said Uwe. "Well, I'll definitely pass the word along to our inspection authorities. It's always been my policy that we strike a balance between public safety and commerce."

With that, Steinberg relaxed. They made small talk for a few minutes about Danish beer and the German legal system. At about twenty after eleven, Steinberg departed.

Uwe ordered in a schnitzel lunch at half past twelve. Ordinarily he would meet with political staffers or lobby groups requesting his ear. But not today. He had kept his slate intentionally clear, to think over what Steinberg actually wanted.

After contemplating Steinberg's known connection to the Israelis, the only possible reason for the lawyer's visit was that the government of Israel was involved in a smuggling operation. So the rumors were probably true.

Two months ago Uwe had asked Dreisler, the man with the crooked nose, to beef up inspections for cargo containers of auto parts coming from Naples. On a hunch he'd gotten from a French naval captain at a fundraiser for Medecins Sans Frontieres.

Of course he knew about the training ground Tel Aviv was using with the Iranians. It was an open secret to everyone in German politics. But the smuggling-that was something different, completely.

Half an hour later, Uwe felt heavy. The schnitzel lunch weighed on his stomach. He decided to go for a walk. Wandering out of the Landtag, he headed for the main commercial area of Kiel.

It was then that things began to feel wrong. Uwe had worked for the BND intelligence service in early 1970s Berlin. His nose could smell when he was being followed.

He looked around the street. Lots of lunchtime crowds still out. Early afternoon shoppers. But he felt someone was following him. He darted in and out of small stores lining Holstenstrasse. Keeping an eye over his shoulder. See who kept themselves constantly in the background.

The fourth store he darted into was a flower shop. By now Uwe was certain he was being pursued by two men in brown leather jackets. Who could they possibly be? They had dark hair. Israelis? Italians? They could even be Americans. It wasn't unusual in this international climate, despite all of Reagan's summit meetings.

Uwe examined a bouquet of tulips when he heard the voice.

"I think your life may be in danger."

Uwe whipped around. A man was standing near a display of carnations.

Mendel. Of course Uwe had no idea of the man's name.

"Who are you to be making such claims?" said Uwe.

"I'm just saying," said Mendel, "that you should play it safe. Not make trouble for a lot of people."

"And who's going to kill me? You?"

"No." Mendel smiled. "I'm just a freelancer. But there are a lot of other people who have problems with you."

Without a further word, Uwe walked out. Leaving the man behind. Outside on the street, the two men in brown leather were nowhere to be seen.

Uwe had a meeting at one-thirty. He refused to feel threatened by some third-rate East German thug that had been hired by the Russians. This hadn't been the first time he'd received death threats. Not even the first time it had happened in person.

Back at the office, he held a meeting with two of his deputies, practicing a speech for later that afternoon.

Later the three of them departed to a press conference at a local market on the other side of town. Uwe got up on a platform and gave a twenty-minute speech. The crowd was small-no more than five or six journalists, and some onlookers.

But for a moment...in the back....

Uwe thought he saw a man with a rifle.

But when he glanced back...nothing. He took a sip of water. Fighting a feeling of panic rising up from his clenched stomach.

By the time he started to take questions he was feeling fine again.

24

By nine o'clock that night, Uwe had finished the day's meetings. And had driven back to Hamburg. The traffic was light going into the city. In just over forty-five minutes he made it to St. Pauli and parked his car across the street from Raven's apartment. Where, unbeknownst to him, every action of his was being surveiled.

He walked up the four flights of stairs and knocked on the door. Raven answered, a cigarette in her hand.

"Well, look. You're here. What could possibly make you deign such a visit?"

He put his fingers to his lips in an effort to keep her quiet while he walked in. As she closed the door, Raven immediately realized something was wrong. She would not have the upper hand in this conversation.

Uwe walked over to the windows and flung the curtains shut, hiding them from observation. Then he went over to Raven's stereo cabinet, selected a Joe Jackson record, and put it on the turntable. When the music started, he turned the volume up full blast.

"What is all this about?" she said stubbing out her cigarette. "Why did you take your clothing from my apartment?"

"I thought you arranged for my wife to break in and steal them."

"What are you talking about?"

"My wife has been in here. She has your address. And photos of us in a compromising position. You don't think that's all an accident, do you?"

The news hit Raven like a sack of bricks. She sat down and put her head in her hands in an attempt to fight off tears. Every bit of resolve she'd steeled over the last few months was breaking down. No matter what, she couldn't admit to Uwe that she worked for the CIA. But what was she going to do now?

Raven stood up, Uwe staring at her as she walked to the kitchen, grabbed a glass and poured in some vodka, followed by orange juice. "Do you want something to drink?" she asked.

"No," he said, "I'm driving."

Raven sipped from her glass. "You came all the way from Kiel to talk to me? Fine. Talk," she demanded. "Tell me what you want me to do."

Uwe moved in to the kitchen so he wouldn't have to yell over the music. "I think my life may be in danger. A man came to see me today. An

130

individual known to work for the East German security services. And sometimes the Russians as well. He might try to talk to you, but I don't want you involved. His name is Mendel."

Raven's back stiffened. "I don't know who that is."

Uwe looked right in her eyes. "You work for the State Department. Maybe you could do some inquiries. Or ask your friends in Bonn."

Raven grinned, uncontrollably. "I don't do that. My job is overseeing passport renewals. Mostly for exchange students and high level managers-"

"Oh, come on," said Uwe. "You don't expect me to believe that?"

"That's my job," said Raven, spilling some of her drink onto the floor. "Shit! Look what you made me do." She grabbed paper towels from a roll near the sink. Anger rose through her as she mopped up the mess. "I don't believe this. You come in here. Start accusing me of things, like I'm some sort of spy-"

"Well, you are? Aren't you?" He glanced toward the windows. "How do I know you weren't sent to seduce me? Maybe your job is to keep an eye on me while your government gets up to no good in my Bundesland."

Raven looked at him coldly. "I think it's time for you to leave."

26

In fact, Uwe was on a rampage.

Raven was shell-shocked when shown the photos. "How could you do this to me?" he said. "Are you having an affair with this man?"

"No. He's just some guy who's been threatening me."

"I don't believe you. This person has pursued both of us." Uwe could barely contain his rage. The photos had arrived on his desk in the late afternoon. Not just showing Mendel entering Raven's apartment, but her having a conversation with the man as she walked him out of the building. How could she be talking to him? The man who told Uwe people were threatening his life?

Raven shook her head. "This makes no sense."

"I don't think I should see you anymore. Maybe you need to be arrested."

"No, this is not what you think it is."

"Then, what is it?" said Uwe.

"It's worse."

"What do you mean?"

"I can't explain."

"Excuse me?"

Raven stood silent.

"Tell me." Uwe pulled her towards him. "Why?"

Raven shuddered, almost in tears. "I can't. Because of national security."

"Who's security? East Germany's?"

"No. But I was sent to make contact with him. I work for the American government. Nothing I've told you has been a lie. My employer is the State Department."

"And our relationship? You don't really love me?"

Raven didn't say anything.

Uwe threw down his hat. "So I see where this leaves us." He grabbed his coat. "Maybe it's a good thing my wife knows about you. All of this is out in the open. It would have been a mistake taking you anywhere on vacation. You're just another person who wants to manipulate power-"

"That's not true. I was asked to follow you. Never was I asked to sleep with you." Raven wiped a tear from her eye. "Or to fall in love with you."

Uwe gazed at her. He would have given everything up for her. But by this point it was just too much to think about trusting Raven ever again. "I don't know what to say about any of this. But I do know this man has threatened me. And now he's seen with you. So it leads me to think you're also threatening me. So if we have contact again, I'll ring the police."

With that he left, slamming the door behind him.

He drove his car back to his house by the river. Hannah was there.

"So you've come back," she said. "Have you decided what we're going to do with the house?"

"I've broken it off. It was all a terrible mistake."

"What do you mean?"

"The other woman. She was betraying me. Perhaps it was a big plot against my career."

Hannah looked at him. She felt sorry for Uwe. He was just so easy to manipulate, wasn't he?

"Why don't we go on holiday?" he asked. "I'll buy you a ticket. We'll go to St. Barts together."

Hannah grimaced. This whole huge mess. "Uwe, look, I don't know. If you need to go-and get away from all these people, get it out of your system-then go off. If you need to take five months and write a book, then go. But if you're to come back to me, I can't handle you like this."

"What do you mean?"

Hannah moved in towards him. "Sit down. Have dinner." She turned around and walked over to the oven, taking out a pot roast. "The school vacation is coming up. I need to be here because Carl and Franke will be back on the eighteenth. After a couple of days we're going down to Geneva to my

135

mother's house. So we'll be there when you get back, alright?"

They ate dinner and Uwe spent the rest of the week in Kiel. Tying up his affairs. Talking to various members of the Landtag that might be interested in taking over from him. He was preparing to leave politics. He called a contact in Bonn to set up a time for him to talk to the corruption committee. Uwe was ready to go public. The staffers were panicked, but he said nothing would impact Chancellor Kohl's government.

He also prepared his resignation letter.

The next Saturday morning he waited for his flight to St. Barts at the Hamburg airport. It was at the gate he felt overwhelmed. With an hour left before takeoff, he walked to a nearby payphone and dialed Raven's number. Mostly out of a feeling of guilt.

But he needn't have felt guilty. The line was already out of service.

27

The distinguishing feature of St. Barthelemy was that it was small. And very far away from pretty much everything. A French overseas department in the Leeward Islands, St. Barts, as it was commonly called by most people, was well known for two things. One, it had a population of less than seven thousand. Which meant it was very difficult to get to because of the small airport. It also had very few places to stay. And very few nosy locals. The second characteristic was that, due to its relative isolation and low population density, it had no television stations. In fact all of the televisions on the island, if you could find one, only received stations from the local cable satellite distributor. None of which were German. Facts that made Uwe happy to be there. It was for this reason the island was so treasured by the world's elite. Unlike, say, more popular destinations like Cuba or the Dominican Republic.

Of course, with the increase in privacy and exclusivity, so went the price of accommodations. Uwe stayed away from the hotels near the main fishing village and had rented a house on the beach, despite the considerable increase in costs. He'd wanted the privacy. And was content to do his own cooking. He was lying on the beach in front of the rented house when he was approached by a journalist. A man named Blake from the New York Times.

They had met each other before. Blake had been posted to Germany two years earlier. He'd interviewed Helmut Kohl several times, as well as several of the party's less prominent members.

"So," said Uwe, "you just happened to be in the neighborhood?"

"No," said Blake, "I requested this assignment. I had some time off coming to me anyway. Figured I could get my flight on the company tab."

"Really?"

"Yes. You're lucky I wanted to come here." Blake looked out over the water. "So what's the big deal?"

"Something is happening." Uwe stood up. "Here, look. You need a drink."

Blake took out his tape recorder. "You don't mind me recording this?"

"As long as it's off the record until I go public."

They went back to the house. Uwe brought out an ice bucket, some Coca-Cola, some lemons and a full bottle of rum. "I'm well stocked here. You'll get the most out of me if we can finish this. Think of it as compensation for not coming back with a story you can publish immediately."

"Fair enough," said Blake. "So, why should anyone care what's going on in Schleswig-Holstein?"

Uwe finished mixing the drinks and handed one to Blake before sitting down and lighting a cigarette. "The Israelis are running guns."

Blake sipped his drink. "That's not exactly news. They run guns everywhere. Not to mention what they're doing with the South Africans."

"Yes, I heard about their nuclear test. But this is different." Uwe took a drag on his cigarette. "I don't have all the background on this. But they're shipping the guns from the port of Ashdod to somewhere in southern Europe. Either Yugoslavia or Italy. I suspect at the port of Naples, because that's where they're paying people off."

"Really?"

"Yes. The local mafia. With the Italian secret service providing the paperwork. And they're shipping weapons all the way through Europe on trucks. Labeled machine parts."

Blake topped up his drink with some Coke. "That's fairly typical."

"They end up at the port of Kiel. There the guns are loaded onto ships. German cargo carriers. That take them to Copenhagen. Then transferred to Iranian-bound vessels. To be shipped to Bandar Abbas."

Blake's face went blank. "You expect me to believe this?"

"I'm telling you, this is what's happening."

"But they're sworn enemies."

Uwe stared at him for a moment too long, as if to express his sentiment that a New York Times reporter could not possibly be so naïve. "Some of the armaments are only good for a guerilla army. So I have a suspicion that whoever is selling these weapons convinced the Israeli leadership that the arms were to be supporting small factions working against the Islamic government."

"But there aren't any successful opposition groups in Iran," said Blake.

"There are Jews in Iran, but none that would ever rise up. And they're certainly not people who would require monthly shipments. Of containerloads of weapons. My opinion is that they started this scheme under the auspices of supporting an Iranian opposition. That is the cover story for arms deals made directly with the Iranian government."

Blake shook his head. "But why? That sounds insane. Shipping weapons to their sworn enemies."

"Who knows? Maybe it's the Mossad? Or Shin Bet? Making money to fund off-the-books operations." Uwe took another swig of his drink. "That was the whole reason behind Iran-Contra. But that's the thing-the weapons didn't stop when Oliver North and his boys were left to hang in the breeze. As long as war is going on, the weapons will flow."

Blake leaned back in his chair. "So why are you going public now?"

"Because the Israelis have run out of luck with the Danes and want to move their shipping operation from Copenhagen to Kiel. Literally within sight of my office. These people-they're completely crazy. They've convinced themselves that anything they do is right. And they don't care who they take down in the process." Uwe chugged back the rest of his drink and poured another. "There's something else you should know. The Israelis are also running a flight school outside Kiel. At an abandoned airfield. They bought cockpit simulators and rented a storage hangar. Brought in some pilots to train the Iranians on the latest Israeli fighter jets."

Blake sipped his drink and gazed out at the setting sun. "You need to go on the record."

"Which I will do as soon as I get back to Germany. Once it's exposed, whoever is selling these weapons will, as you Americans say, shit a brick. I'm willing to bet these arms sales were approved by an Israeli government bill of sale that was granted under false pretenses. For the politicians it will make for difficult explanations."

"And you brought me here for a backgrounder?"

"You're going to need it," said Uwe. "This mess is extraordinarily complicated. All this spy stuff. It's a wilderness of mirrors."

28

The call came late in the morning. A long conference call with the people at Langley. By the end MacLean knew that nothing would stay the same. He couldn't decide if his wife would be overjoyed or terrified by the fact he was moving back home.

The next day, just after lunch, Raven arrived at his office.

"Well," she said after greeting him, "you haven't given me enough time to deal with this whole Mendel thing."

"It's over."

"What do you mean?"

"We're over. We're done here. You're through with your boyfriend anyway, right?"

"I don't understand. What are you talking about?"

"You've been transferred. And so have I. Both of us to headquarters. I've requested you in my office.

That pretty much kept you from being shipped back to Guinea-Bissau."

Mixed feelings flooded through Raven. Part of her had hoped the whole situation with Uwe could be worked out. "But you know, I'd really like to see where this goes. Some viable leads will be left hanging."

"Which will be dealt with. By the Bonn station."

"But they have no one in Hamburg-"

"They have a consulate there. If they think it's worth their while, I'm sure they can send up somebody."

"So you set me up to get some usable intelligence from this guy, but when I finally make some headway, you rip me away?"

MacLean looked at her, not quite believing what he was hearing. "You said you wanted to be put back in Washington. Both of us have family there. You'll have a cushy job and no tropical diseases to worry about." MacLean leaned forward. "I think it's in both of our interests if we forgot about this thing with Berlioz. Pursuing Mendel may put blood on both of our hands."

"Uwe knows about our relationship with Mendel. He's fearful his life may be in danger."

"Nonsense. Nobody would kill a sitting German politician. But his family-that's another story."

Raven's eyes widened. "What do you mean?"

"I just read a communication saying the Iranians have been keeping a surveillance team on his wife.

They might try to go after her in Geneva."

"What?"

"They might try to take out the wife or one of his children."

"Are you going to tell the police?"

MacLean grinned. "Tell them what? All we've got are suspicions. And coded signals that could have been mistranslated from Farsi. There's a good chance they'll do nothing. The Iranians usually only take action if they feel they've been wronged." MacLean opened up a file in front of him. "This guy Mendel has a resume a mile long. He works mostly for the communists in East Berlin, but he's also connected to a white supremacist group with connections to the KKK in Oklahoma. And he runs terrorist seminars with Muslim extremists in the Philippines. Takes Europeans and Americans down there to learn how to blow up buildings. Crazy stuff like that." MacLean closed the file. "Either way, you should stay out of it. This kind of business has plenty of false leads. You don't want to get involved."

Raven went cold. "No. I suppose I don't."

"The office on the second floor has your transfer papers ready. MI6 will also need to book you out of the safe house."

"When do I ship out?"

"You still have a couple of weeks to go," said MacLean. "Think of it like a paid vacation. In Germany."

On the flight back to Hamburg Raven mulled over her situation. All she felt for Uwe was a certain numbness. It had been wrong for her to get emotionally attached to someone she was using for information.

That night she got back to the apartment. She found the envelope with her airplane ticket to St. Barts. And a piece of paper with the contact info for the house Uwe had booked.

Including the phone number.

Shutting the curtains and turning out the lights, she left. Took the S-Bahn to the Hamburg Hauptbanhof. Bought an international phone card and dialed the number to Uwe's vacation rental. It would be just before dinnertime there.

"Hello?" said Uwe.

"It's me," said Raven.

'I don't want to talk to you."

"Your wife is in danger. In Geneva. That's all you need to know."

Raven hung up and hurried back home.

29

It was mid-afternoon when the phone rang. Raven sat at her kitchen table. Smoking a cigarette after finishing a cup of coffee.

Mendel's voice was on the line. "Something is about to happen. You'd better go to Geneva."

"Why? I see no reason to trust you."

"Then don't. But I know all about your relationship to Uwe Berlioz."

"Stop playing games."

"Go to Geneva. Stay at the Hotel de la Paix. Under your real name. I'll contact you there tonight."

Shivers went through Raven's spine. She sat down, and thought about what to do. Should she contact MacLean? But they were off this file. The CIA would probably want to send another operative, if they did anything at all. No, she had to do this herself. Even if it meant risking her life.

She took the bus to Hamburg airport. Got the first available flight out. Night had already fallen when she got to Geneva. She checked in to the Hotel de la Paix and waited.

It was half past two when Mendel phoned her.

"This will probably be our final communication," he said. "Think of it as a favor from me."

"What have your people done?"

"Oh no, this time it's not me. Or anyone associated with me. It's one of yours. Or at least one of your so-called allies. An Israeli Kidon squad has visited Mr. Berlioz. Unfortunately they made one big mistake. With the bottle of wine."

"What are you talking about?"

"He ordered a bottle of wine."

"Where? In St. Barts?"

"No, you fool. He's in Geneva. Room 388 at the Des Bergues Hotel. He ordered an obscure bottle of wine. But he'll never get to finish drinking it. Your friends replaced it with the wrong vintage to cover their tracks."

"You're speaking in riddles."

"Remember, this is on your side." Mendel hung up.

Raven put on her coat. Grabbed a small tool she used for picking locks. And went to the Des Bergues Hotel. It was three in the morning when she got to room 388. Putting her ear to the door, she listened. Just the low-level noise of a TV. She took her lock-picking tool and got the door open. She didn't have much time. Room service would be distributing morning papers soon.

Inside, all the lights were on. The bed hadn't been slept in. Raven's senses came alive. She carefully closed the door behind her. On a table by the window she saw a room service tray. A bottle of pinot noir. The bed hadn't been slept in, but it appeared someone had ruffled up the bedspread.

Then she turned to the bathroom.

Shock overwhelmed her. It felt like she was crumbling. Nausea filled her gut.

Uwe.

Naked.

In the bathtub.

Under the water. His eyes bulging with death.

Raven felt tears welling in her eyes.

She had to leave. A black American woman at a murder scene in central Europe-not a good thing. Her mind shut off all emotion. And focused on getting out. Quietly she opened the door, checked the hallway, and walked away. Took the stairs to the second floor. Then got the elevator to the lobby.

When she got back to her hotel room, she poured herself a glass of vodka from the mini-bar and began to cry.

Part Three

From Chicago, Washington, and Montreal to the Afghan border

1987

30

There was nothing but blackness. Gradually Joshua became aware that his foot was numb. He woke up. Looked down at his legs. Saw they were twisted at an odd angle. He rolled over. Straightened out. Nothing was broken. He lay back. Looked at the sky. He'd never seen it so blue. With such fluffy clouds drifting by. Like cotton candy.

He lay there for a while. Listened to the sound of his breathing. It took him a while before he realized he was in an open field. A grassy field. No longer in the CERN collider. What had happened? Had he been stunned? Some sort of electromagnetic shock? Maybe he'd got to one of the evac tubes. Scrambled out of the complex. Fallen asleep outside. It certainly looked like the area outside CERN. Except there were no hills.

Joshua sat up. Panic stricken. How long have I been lying here? he wondered. Feeling his pockets, he found his iPhone and his wallet. His car keys were back in the gulag. He had the AC adapter and his headphones.

Okay. Everything's going to be okay. He just had to get back to the campus. They were probably looking for him anyway. Probably panicked. The police might have been called. Or worse.

He stood up. Saw buildings in the distance. No part of the CERN campus looked like this. It was just too flat. No farms around. Joshua checked his phone. It said nine-thirty-eight at night. That seemed right. He'd got to the gulag right after nine. But it was broad daylight.

Joshua turned around. In the distance he saw some white buildings. "Well," he mumbled to himself, "that's where I've got to go."

He started to walk.

31

The buildings were blocked by a large chain-link fence. Joshua had to walk around the edge of the tree line. This led to a wide four-lane road, which was surprisingly devoid of traffic. He found a parking lot.

Then he saw the sign: "Fermilab. A project of the University of Chicago."

Chicago? How the hell?

He walked to the front entrance, but the doors were locked. As Joshua turned around a bus pulled in. He got on.

"Student card, please."

"Um, ahhh...." Joshua looked at the route map. This bus was headed to the Hyde Park campus. "Jeeze, I forgot mine at my residence."

"Fine, get on. You don't look familiar, though."

"I...uh...just moved here from Europe." He walked to the back of the bus and sat down.

32

A tiredness overwhelmed Joshua. Like nothing he'd ever felt in his entire life. The moment he sat down he closed his eyes. When he woke up he was still the only passenger, but they were well into the Hyde Park neighborhood of Chicago. On a narrow commercial street. All the buildings were old, run down. Something was definitely off. The signs on the stores. Was it the font?

He looked down at the pedestrians on the sidewalk.

Punks.

With enormous purple Mohawk hairdos.

Wow, he thought. He hadn't been to Chicago in a long time. Things must have really changed in the last couple years. You'd never see someone dressed like that in Europe. Let alone Los Alamos.

Then he saw the cars.

Crown Victorias. Jesus, everything's a Crown Vic. This neighborhood has turned seriously ghetto. Then he saw a Chrysler Reliant. A K-car! What the hell? How did they keep those on the road? All the cars, they all looked like they were from the seventies. Or the sixties. This couldn't be right. He saw a hideously-yellow Toyota, the kind he remembered from his childhood.

A group of women walked down the street, past the punks. The dresses...they looked to be fifty percent shoulder pads.

Then up in the sky.

A billboard.

An advertisement.

For Michael Jackson's 'Bad' album.

33

The bus stopped.

"Hey, buddy," yelled the driver. "This is the last stop. Main campus."

Joshua stumbled out of the bus, onto a mostly empty campus. It must be Sunday. He was hungry. And, curiously enough, he really wanted a drink.

There was only one place he knew would be open at this time of day, if it was the weekend.

34

Joshua wandered through the campus. Found Ida Noyes Hall. An old gothic-style building. He wandered into the concrete foyer. Clomped down a set of stairs to the basement. Passing through a set of doors the decor went from faux-European to Midwestern dive bar.

This was the campus pub. The only one, as far as Joshua knew. He had spent plenty of time down here during the two years of his master's degree. It wasn't much, but he remembered it having a good selection of beers on tap.

The room was completely deserted except for two preppy-looking gentlemen seated at the bar. Dressed like Alex P. Keaton from Family Ties. The quintessential 1980s situation comedy. It was a uniform of khakis, sweaters, and neckties. On either side the stools were occupied by hard plastic briefcases, draped with sports jackets.

"But Friedman is unequivocal," said the first Alex P. Keaton. "If a business is run poorly, it should be left to fail."

"Yeah," said the second, "but then you create negative expectations for the economy as a whole. While shock therapy is important-"

"No, it's everything. It gives the politicians cover. To allow them to enact reforms. And enforce spending cuts. You're making monetary rule."

"But the Keynesian point of view has some benefits."

"Have you run the math? Have you seen how the econometric models work? It's not pretty. You have to just cut, get rid of all the regulation."

"I agree, but think of all those old people who'll get angry. They vote."

"Screw the old people. They should've saved more money. And, with less regulation, they can keep working."

Joshua leaned on the bar. An attractive blond girl emerged from the back.

"Hey," he said, moving away from the two Alex P. Keaton types, "is there a wi-fi spot near here? My phone can't get on to the network."

She looked at him blankly. "Huh?"

"I just wanted to get on the internet. To check my email."

"Email? E...e...e...?"

"Electronic mail."

She finally understood. "Oh, I know that. I'm only first year computer science. But the cook is a senior. He'll know about that stuff." She disappeared into the back.

Joshua smiled. A little bit too widely. What the hell was wrong with this girl? He sighed and looked down at the beer menu. Pabst Blue Ribbon. He was starving. Please tell me there's food here, he thought. He grabbed a newspaper lying on the counter nearby. Glanced at the headlines.

Baby Jessica rescued from well.

Ronald Reagan agrees to summit meeting with Gorbachev.

Was this paper some sort of joke? Joshua turned to the sports page.

A full page story on John McEnroe.

The TV section had a feature on Star Trek: The Next Generation.

He turned back to the front page.

The Chicago Sun-Times. Sunday edition. October 18th, 1987.

From behind the counter the bartender appeared. "So, yeah," she said, "I know how to help you. You just go out the front of this building. And turn right. The third building down. The lab is in the basement."

Joshua's hand was shaking.

"Are you okay?"

"Nothing. It's just jet lag. I just...ah...flew in from Geneva."

"Sure."

He gazed into her eyes. "This paper, it's a joke, right? A campus humor mag?"

"Well, I think all of Reagan's politics are a joke." She looked down at the headlines. "Oh, yeah, that baby in the well. So sad."

"This is today's paper?"

"Yup. We get it every day." She looked at him. "Do you want a beer, or something? I hate to break it to you, but the bar's only for university staff and students. You have to pay for cover, and need to be accompanied by someone."

"Yeah, umm...."

"It's fifty cents. Otherwise I'm not supposed to serve you."

Joshua nodded. Then something occurred to him. "Uh, yes. You're absolutely right. I'm supposed to meet one of the faculty here. But they're late. Do you have a telephone I could use? I don't have any American money."

"Yeah, sure." She leaned back and grabbed an old-style rotary phone. And a skinny campus phone book. "It's a direct line anywhere on campus."

Joshua opened the directory. Think about it. It's 1987. The University of Chicago. Fermilab.

He opened the book to 'S'. Found the number and began dialing.

35

"I'm afraid you've come here on false pretenses, Mr. Sinclair." Axel Straussbecker reached for the phone on his desk.

"Wait...don't call the police."

Joshua had convinced the grad student answering the phone that he was a doctoral candidate from England. That had gotten him through the door. But Axel, even this young version of himself, free of wrinkles and grey hairs, was not so easily won over. This Axel couldn't be more than a few years older than Joshua. He had been cordial at first, but as the story was blurted out, a look of concern appeared on his face.

Joshua gazed around the office. It was a shock seeing the younger Axel. He was devoid of the bitterness he showed every day at CERN. The feeling that he'd had his time. Hell, this was his time, wasn't it?

Then there was the room. Axel's CERN office didn't have a loose piece of paper floating around. But this place...it looked like little more than a storage closet with a small window at forehead level. Barely wide enough for a desk and a chalkboard. Every other available space was occupied by journals, textbooks or notes waiting to be filed.

Joshua considered himself lucky Axel was even at the office on a Sunday. "Look," he said, "I understand you don't believe me-"

Axel reached for the phone receiver.

"Wait-I can prove it."

Joshua dug his iPhone out of his pocket.

36

"Remarkable. Absolutely remarkable."

They were watching Back to the Future on Joshua's iPhone. For all those people who thought he was stupid to download movies to his phone, he finally had an answer.

Axel was awestruck. "An entire library of movies...on a telephone."

"Well, it's not much of a library, but...if you had a wireless internet connection-"

"A what connection?"

"Internet. I mean ARPANET. Or whatever connects the computers to the mainframe."

"Wireless?"

"Yes. We don't use telephone lines in the future. It's just...in the air. You can access pretty much any video ever made, if it's been uploaded."

"What do you mean, uploaded?"

Joshua spent the next ten minutes explaining the concept of Youtube. Before giving up.

Axel examined the phone's menu. "It has everything. A calculator. A calendar. Maps." He punched the map icon. It displayed only grey.

"You have to have a connection for it to work. Most of the data isn't stored on the phone."

"I see. And what is this 'mail' program? Does the post office no longer deliver door-to-door in the future?"

Joshua smiled. "We do, but...."

"And this text message button? Is this some sort of telegram machine?"

"Kind of...."

"My god. Tell me, this time you're from...is it everything we'd imagined in the Stanley Kubrick film? With moon colonies?"

"Um, no. But we do have Skype, which is a kind of videophone. And it's free."

"I must know-do they have flying cars?"

"No. Everyone drives trucks."

Axel seemed disappointed by that.

"But," said Joshua, "we have electronic books."

"People still read books in the future?"

"Some do."

"Wow." Axel sat down, pondering everything he'd just been shown. "This technology. How could I possibly be of any use to you?"

"Well," said Joshua, embarrassed to be asking, "I need a place to stay."

37

Axel drove up to the front of the Royal Castle Motel. As far as Joshua could see, it was neither royal nor castle.

They had driven to the south Chicago location in Axel's 1984 Chevrolet Monte Carlo. Joshua took a perverse delight in a car that was at the same time hideously old and almost new. What surprised him was how the vehicle, even in the late eighties, already seemed out of date with many of the smaller Japanese cars on the road. They took the highway from Hyde Park. But the moment they got off to the side streets Joshua was stuck by the degree of urban blight. He remembered Chicago being rough, but it seemed even worse in the past.

Axel put the car in park. The hotel's exterior was done up in a tacky castle motif. Faux-stone siding, the type popularized in the sixties and seventies.

Wood paneling. The neighborhood was dotted with check-cashing places and pawn shops.

Axel took out his wallet. Handed some bills to Joshua. "Here's two hundred dollars. That should keep you going for a few days."

"Thanks."

"I'll be back around three-thirty tomorrow to pick you up. Please be ready. Not that you'd want to leave your room in this neighborhood."

"Not the nicest place, is it?" He pulled on the door handle, pushing away the enormous slab of metal and fabric. He had forgotten how heavy car doors used to be. He stopped before he got out. "Just one thing."

"Yes," said Axel.

"I really shouldn't tell you this...."

Axel raised an eyebrow. "Then you should keep your mouth shut."

"It really doesn't matter. It's Sunday. The markets are closed."

"What? Do you have a hot stock tip? You keep all of that in your head?"

Joshua stared out through the windscreen. "I know you don't think I'm from the future. Everything I've shown you could be argued against. Like, by someone who thinks I'm with the army or something."

Axel remained silent.

"Or maybe you think I'm some sort of whack job."

"I'm trying to believe your story. Either way, what you've shown me-"

"Tomorrow will be the single worst day on the stock market since 1929. By the end of this month, a number of foreign stock exchanges will lose half their value."

"Are you saying our entire economy is going to collapse overnight?"

"No, but trust me. It's going to be a bloodbath. If I were you, the moment you get up I'd sell everything."

Axel smiled. "Then I don't have to worry. I have no money to lose."

38

Early the next day, Axel sat in the main room of his front office. He shared it with several other researchers. And graduate students, who were loath to show up early on a Monday morning. He had arrived a couple hours earlier, getting some work done on their new desktop computer. It came with a full printer setup, which meant the people in the lab no longer had to trek over to the computer science building when they needed to get a hard copy.

Axel hit print on the computer. The dot matrix printer made an ugly racket. He wandered over to the office of Marjorie, the department's secretary.

"Good morning."

"Morning, professor. Hope you don't have any stocks."

"Why?"

"Listen." She reached over and turned up the radio.

"The continuing carnage came as a shock," said the announcer. "After markets in Asia began shedding early this morning, the Dow followed suit, down four hundred points. With the continued slide some have called on Treasury Secretary James Baker to call a halt to trading."

Axel leaned over and turned off the radio. His face was ashen. He walked out of the room, leaving Marjorie with the impression he'd lost a lot of money.

Returning to his small private office, he closed the door and collapsed into the chair behind his desk. There was no doubting Joshua's story. Some part of him wanted to believe that he was a kook. Or a genius engineer. But this...this was evidence. Even if it contradicted everything they knew about physics. He looked down at the page he had printed out. A year ago, none of this math had existed. Maybe, thirty years from now, they'd devised a way of going back in time.

The only way to deal with this was through the proper scientific method. Follow a procedure. Axel reached for his rolodex. Confirming Joshua's story, if possible, would need work. He picked up the phone and talked to the Fermilab collider scheduling office.

39

Axel's Monte Carlo was waiting in front of the hotel lobby promptly at three thirty. Joshua walked out and hopped in the passenger side.

"How was you stay?"

"Terrible," said Joshua. "A prostitute rented the room next door. She had clients in and out all night."

"You didn't knock? Or complain? Maybe get her services for free?"

"I just turned up my television. For the most part, it wasn't so bad. Despite the thin walls. Most of the customers were in and out. But a couple times she had these talkers. I don't even think they had sex. Just a guy rambling for half an hour. And I had to listen to it."

Axel turned toward Interstate 94. Traffic was backed up toward the on-ramp. "Look, I'm sorry to have doubted you-"

"So you saw the news?"

"Yeah. I spent the morning working out a plan. Talked to the hospital. We need to get some samples. Check for radiation poisoning."

"That's the strange thing." Joshua lowered his window, letting the cool breeze flow in. "We had Geiger counters in the collider. To the very end, we've never seen radiation. No matter how high the volume of energy we pump through there."

"I spent some time studying up on the various theories of superstrings-"

"Oh, uh, yeah, about that, they were all combined in 1995."

"What?"

"Yeah. We see them all as the same thing, just from different mathematical perspectives."

"I see, but even so, to test such propositions in a laboratory setting would require amounts of power we could never hope to generate. At Fermilab, or anywhere."

"Well now, that's the mystery, isn't it? Because neither can the collider at CERN. Something happened, at a string level, without requiring huge amounts of energy. My presence here indicates that something in the mathematics is wrong."

"Probably." Axel turned onto the highway. "Do you have any documents on your phone that could help me brush up on what you've discovered in the next thirty years?"

"Maybe." Joshua put up his window as they accelerated.

"Look, I've talked to my wife. We've got a spare room in the basement."

"Did you...?

"No. She thinks you're a graduate student who needs an apartment. So you're good for the next couple of months. But at some point you'll need a birth certificate. And you might want to get a job."

"What do you want to do today?"

"I'll drop you at the hospital. You need some blood work done. Can you find your way back to my lab after that? I'm assuming the campus hasn't changed much in the future."

At the hospital Joshua went to the second floor. The reception desk at the blood clinic was waiting for him. He was escorted to a room, but stopped at the doorway. The nurse was helping an emaciated man get into a wheelchair.

As the man was rolled out, Joshua took his seat. The nurse looked over. "You don't want to sit there, sir."

"Why?"

The nurse leaned in, lowered her voice. "That man has AIDS. We usually disinfect-"

"It's okay. I'm sure he's not contagious."

The nurse looked at him and shook her head before walking away.

The blood tech came back. She was a pretty blond girl. Perfectly Midwestern. "My name's Trish."

Joshua introduced himself.

"So, you work with the physics department?"

"Yeah. We're still waiting to hear back on my grant application."

"They have that big collider, out on the edge of town, right?"

"Yeah, Fermilab. I suppose I'll be working there."

Trish prepared a syringe. "How long have you been in Chicago?"

"Since yesterday. But I did some graduate work here a few years ago."

"I see."

"Can I ask you a question?"

"Sure."

"Is everyone in this hospital terrified of AIDS?"

Trish hesitated, not knowing what to say. "I'm not. But a lot of people are. The south side is poor. Since we're a research hospital, we get a lot of the worst cases. People don't know what to think. All these men...they're dying. And we can't do anything. The president won't even acknowledge AIDS exists. A lot of them are angry about that. Not that most of them would vote for Reagan anyway. All he cares about is communism."

"That's on its way out."

Trish finished taking the blood sample and applied a Band-Aid. "I hope so." She grabbed a pair of scissors from a nearby table. "Now, I just need a sample of your hair."

40

The Fermilab control room was a hell of a lot smaller than the one at CERN. To Joshua, it felt like everything here was the complete opposite. He couldn't get over that the room had almost no video displays of any kind. Computer screens didn't exist. Instead, they had a wall of knobs, buttons, and dials. All different sorts. Each regulating a separate component of the beam power.

It was cramped, too.

Joshua found a spot behind Axel and a man named Stirling, the collider technician. It felt crowded. A lone black and white video feed from the tunnel displayed on a television in the corner of the room. The lone visual reference. The nearest computer was ten floors above them. Above the bank of dials were waveforms and oscillators. It reminded Joshua of an electrical engineering lab he had frequented as an undergrad. The atmosphere was very, very strange.

Still, it was kind of exciting. Many things hummed and beeped.

"So," said Stirling, "we're ready to start the experiment in a few minutes. I'm just waiting for—" A bell on a nearby control panel rang. Stirling picked up a telephone receiver. "Yes? Thank you." He turned to Axel and Joshua. "The generator station has confirmed voltage. We're ready to go."

Alex leaned over and nodded to the technician. The young man responded by standing up and flipping a giant red switch on a panel above him. Sitting down, he turned his attention to a large dial. Correcting the beam.

Axel began a countdown. "Five...four...three... two...one...."

Stirling nodded. "Executing." The dial went higher and higher. Lights on the console illuminated, some of them flashing. A waveform scope lit up. Similar to the oscillation monitor he watched in the CERN control room. Although far more rudimentary. The tech adjusted a bunch of dials. Getting the beam to smooth out.

On the video feed, Joshua watched a small vial of his blood. It had been placed right in the path of the beam. As the energy impacted, it seemed like a shine came over the vial.

"Great," he said, looking around the room. "So where do we view the results? What monitor do they show up on?"

"Monitor?" said Stirling. "What are you talking about?"

"We have to get the film developed first," said Axel.

Joshua was confused. "The what?"

"The particles register on various emulsion films. It's how we measure if the collider beam has made an impact. We also have a printout scan machine-" He indicated to a large roll of paper to his right. "This shows us the amount of energy being created."

"So how long will it take to get the results?"

"We should have them pretty quickly," said Axel. "Within forty-eight hours."

Joshua stifled a gasp. At CERN the same process took about forty-eight seconds.

41

The office hadn't been redecorated since 1976. And Richard Auburn was well aware of it. The wood paneling on the wall behind his desk ended halfway to the floor, giving way to yellow and brown plaid wallpaper. He wished someone would put in a requisition for renovations. He'd do it himself were it not for the fact that it looked self-serving. At least he was high enough up in the hierarchy to get his own office. But hell, this entire floor was due for an update.

Auburn walked over to his window, looking out at the grassy field that surrounded the building. Didn't move when he heard the door to his office open and shut. He just stood there, looking out at the grassy fields that surrounded the complex. In the far distance he spotted a man with a lawn mower.

Now in his mid-fifties, Auburn had long since been using a dye in the shower to maintain his hair a perfect chestnut color. In a suit and tie he was the perfect model of a high level civil servant. One of the reasons he hated dealing with the military. He always had to make sure they knew who the boss was.

Hearing a throat clearing behind him, Auburn finally turned around. Stared at Major Jack MacLean. Auburn silently moved across the room and sat down behind his desk. Didn't even say hello. Just picked up a file folder and opened it. "I expected disaster when you were assigned here, but not this."

MacLean's eyes drifted around the office. Landing on a picture of Auburn shaking hands with President Reagan. Placed as close to the edge of the desk as possible. A reminder of who you were talking to.

Auburn flipped through some sheets of paper. "Just pissing away our budget."

MacLean shifted in his chair. He wanted to growl. "With all due respect, sir-"

"Major, a congressional oversight committee may have forced you on me, but that doesn't mean I'm blind and stupid to your antics."

MacLean rolled his eyes. He'd been dealing with twerps like this guy Auburn his whole career. Ever since he'd moved out of military intelligence, into a position working with the CIA. Almost two years ago now.

With all his practical duties in Europe, this was his first week back in Washington. And they'd stuck him with this asshole. The kind of guy who he'd doubted would give him more than a second glance at a staff meeting.

Auburn swiveled around, turning to gaze out the

window. "That whole fiasco with your buddy Oliver North last year...."

MacLean felt anger rising inside of him. "That had nothing to do with me."

"Quit it. Save it for confession."

So that was what it was, thought MacLean. It was all about a witch hunt. Find out who the bad guys were. Auburn had been left out of the loop when everything had gone down with the Iranians. Now he had to poke and probe all through the entire department. It didn't really matter much. MacLean had plenty of connections to congress. To all of the subcommittees who were responsible for allocating the CIA's budget. So even though Auburn was the superior in the chain of command, MacLean had much more sway with the politicians who oversaw the show. Auburn knew that. But he still wasn't going to put up with military bullshit. "I'd just like to know," he said, "what you're doing down there as our military liaison."

Auburn looked down and flicked through the papers in front of him.

MacLean stood up. Uncomfortable with whatever documents Auburn had in there. Began to pace back and forth.

"Let's start with your travel record for the last year. In December you made five trips to Managua—"

He didn't get to finish the sentence. Auburn's office door slammed shut.

Holy fuck. MacLean just walked out.

42

The slam of the papers on the desk stirred up a whirlwind.

Axel turned around. From the blackboard, where he was working through a series of Joshua's equations.

"This isn't good enough."

Axel put down his chalk. Quietly he moved over to his chair. "Sit down."

Joshua dragged out the flimsy wooden seat. It was old and uncomfortable. The kind of chair usually stacked away. Not meant for long bouts of sitting. Suitable more for a church hall.

Axel leaned forward. "I understand how you're frustrated. I'm starting to believe your story myself."

"Starting?" Joshua slumped back in despair. What would it take to convince Axel? Joshua knew this situation was completely ridiculous. But there had to be something that would get rid of the doubt that lingered over every conversation, as if Joshua was some kind of crazy person.

"I'm dealing with limited resources. An army of administrators are asking about my use of Fermilab, okay? It's one of the few institutions in the entire world capable of carrying out these kinds of experiments. Maybe in the year 2017 you have one of these on every street corner, but in the here and now, we don't." Axel sighed. "Our understanding of physics has advanced faster than we ever imagined. But—"

"Yeah, yeah," said Joshua, looking at the blackboard. He would never have taken this tone of voice with the elderly Axel. But seeing him at a time when they were the same age made him far less tolerant of his bullshit.

Axel picked up a pen and began tapping it against a nearby notepad. "You said you don't really understand the mechanism that brought you here. And all we have available is 1980s technology."

Joshua shook his head. "That's not the issue. This can be done. We're not doing anything fundamentally different thirty years in the future. Whatever happened to me can be re-created at this facility. I'm certain of it."

"Even if we could build a device to send you through time, what if a mad man got a hold of it? And gave Hitler a nuclear warhead? Or Napoleon a machine gun?"

"That's nonsense."

"Is it? And...." Axel struggled to find the correct words in English. "Even at the rate we're progressing, there's no guarantee that we won't hit a wall. You understand? We only have so much computational power. There's no way to run these equations as you would in the supercomputers of your era." Axel turned to the blackboard. "Even this thing on the wall here.... To calculate all the permutations could take weeks. Multiply that by all the maths and dimensions these equations evoke.... You end up with some real problems. Everything takes too much time. There's not enough resources."

"What are you trying to say, then?"

Axel shook his head. "It might be faster to get you to 2017 by waiting it out."

Joshua stood up, putting his hands on Axel's desk. "So you're not even willing to try?"

"I'm not opposed to trying. I've got the time and the equipment. But these are very expensive toys we're playing with. They use a lot of electricity. Without a grant application...."

Joshua narrowed his gaze. "This is a money thing?"

"Basically, yes."

"Why didn't you say so?"

Axel looked confused. As if the financial factor should be obvious to anyone.

Joshua smiled. "How much do you need?"

43

Few things angered MacLean more than the office he'd been given upon his transfer to Langley.

In Bonn, he'd had an extensive room to stretch out in. The U.S. Army had practically constructed a small city along the river in Plittersdorf. Custom built after the war. Since Bonn was such a small town, there had been lots of space to build. Offices were big. The entire community was there to provide for American bureaucrats. Hell, you could even buy a frozen turkey at a reasonable price. Try doing that somewhere else in Europe. It was well regarded as one of the more luxurious embassy compounds throughout the world.

Now that he was back in the continental United States, no one was going out of their way to give a Major anything more than might be expected at his rank. They had allotted him one of the few spare offices in the building. Claimed they had to keep people in silos, so they had no other space available. Not to mention the fact that the military brass were somewhat distrusted in this building.

The one bright spot about the room was that it was good for playing darts.

On the far wall, by the door, hung a small calendar. MacLean grabbed one of the green-tailed projectiles from his desk. Fired it at the wall. It landed right on today's date-November 12, 1987.

A smile crossed his face.

That was the game he'd invented. The bulls eye was whatever the day was. Just as he was about to aim a second dart, the door burst open.

Raven came in. In her hand a large bright red file. And a full head of steam.

"You're interrupting my game," said MacLean.

Raven slammed the door behind her. MacLean looked her over, wondering what had gotten into his new bureau chief. In the three months since the death of Uwe Berlioz, she had recovered from the stress of the operation quite admirably. But MacLean knew that Raven was only happy when she had something to sink her teeth into. An assignment of substance. And it looked like she'd found it.

"Can you keep a secret?" she said.

"You're in the way of my dart board."

She didn't budge. "Can I tell you what I heard, or not?"

"What?"

Raven glared at him, the gaze reserved only for serious matters. In his time working in the intelligence community, MacLean had pretty much seen it all. Nothing that would cross Raven's desk here could possible warrant his interest. Not unless he already heard about it from someone upstairs. Nonetheless, he relented. "Fine. Calm down. Take a seat."

She sat down. "There's a real shit-storm brewing around you."

"That is not a secret."

"Rumor has it that Auburn dropped your name during one of his regular briefings to the president. And it wasn't to sing your praises."

"This is why you burst in here? You're so excited to tell me what a terrible job I'm doing?"

"I may have something that could save your ass." Raven passed him the red file folder.

MacLean noted it was marked 'Eyes Only.' "What is all this?"

"A friend of mine from college got a job with the S. E. C. last year. I was in New York last weekend, so we met for lunch. She told me about some unusual stock market activity."

"What's unusual about a stock market crash? I lost a shitload of money."

Raven stood up and leaned forward, her arms propped on MacLean's desk. "You don't understand. How about someone making a shitload of money in a bear market?"

"Doesn't sound like a crime to me."

"Take a look."

MacLean gave her a begrudging glance and opened the folder. "Is this something to do with a foreign agent or a Soviet plot?"

"It could. That's the question. Maybe this'll let you win one for the gipper."

44

Velour was the favorite material of Marianne, Axel's wife.

Every piece of furniture she'd bought in America was covered with it. Fortunately, Axel had managed to confine her ambitions to the living room.

Joshua sat down on the matching love seat that occupied the corner of the room. The house was in Arlington Heights, one of the more walkable suburbs of Chicago. But it was certainly far away from the university. There was just no way Axel could afford to live that close to Hyde Park. And the parts of it they could afford, they didn't want to live. On the bright side, from Axel's house it was a lot easier to get to Batavia, where Fermilab was located.

Today Joshua was entertaining a man named Ray Coates. He'd arrived from J.P. Morgan fifteen minutes previous. He'd brought with him a summary of Axel and Joshua's financial activities over the last three weeks.

Coates was an overweight stockbroker with a small mop of blond hair that matched his mustache. He seemed well-meaning, although it was clear he'd never seen anything like the profits generated in his new account. Even so, the man had a nervous demeanor. Joshua wondered if the guy suspected they were doing something illegal.

But that was impossible.

There was no way such a permutation of random trades would ever cause the federal government to suspect anything.

Axel walked in with a tea set and placed it down on the coffee table. The ornate silver of the tea set clashed against the tacky 70s-style southwest furniture. Purchased at the very start of the decade, it seemed. A time when country music had displaced disco.

Coates shifted his open briefcase out of the way to make room for the tea set.

Axel poured. "Sugar?"

"Yes, please," said the stockbroker.

Once everyone had a mug of tea, Coates took out a dot-matrix printout of four or five hundred sheets from his briefcase. He handed the papers to Joshua. "So you see what we're talking about. There are certainly substantial costs to all the trades you've been making. But I've never seen someone so able to take advantage of a bear market the way you have."

Joshua looked at the paper. "It's unbelievable."

"I agree," said Coates. "It is an exceptional run of trades you've made."

"I'm talking about all the dead trees," said Joshua, shaking his head. "You took the time to print all this out?"

"You're an unbelievable customer. I've never seen someone take two million dollars and turn it into a hundred and twenty million in such a record time. Not legitimately, anyway." Coates dabbed at his brow. "I'm sure all your funding has been completely legitimate, hasn't it?" Beads of sweat dripped down his forehead.

Axel put his mug down. "Of course. It is all above the bar. We have not been performing bank heists here." He stood up and began to pace.

"Tell me, Mr. Coates, how many people are aware of our...situation?"

"Just me and the managing partners."

"I'm sure discretion is your top priority." Axel tapped at his lower lip. "Your firm is collecting quite a windfall in stock trading fees, isn't it?"

"Sure is. Actually, we've been talking. Wondering if you might consider working for us. Put your knowledge to use. I understand working for a university-"

"Please, Mr. Coates." Axel shook his head. "It seems mathematics has a lot to offer a stockbroker like yourself. But this was a one time thing. Do us all a favor and give your dreams of avarice a rest."

"If there's anybody else out there who can do this...imagine if we took all the people like yourselves...people with degrees in physics and mathematics and engineering. And got them to work on the stock market? Think of the money we'd make."

"I know exactly what that would be like," said Joshua, looking up from the spreadsheet. "It would be a disaster."

Coates looked at him disbelievingly. "How can you say something like that? These modeling techniques I've heard you can do are fantastic. And so are the computers we have today."

Joshua smiled. "I'm sure you make a whole lot of profit. But we all know, you can only make the big money if you're willing to take on a whole lot of risk." Joshua put down the spreadsheet. The tea set silver clanged as the mass of paper slammed onto the table. "Listen, tell me something.... How liquid are these finances?"

"Completely liquid. You can turn them into cash at any time. But the hit you'll take from the taxman-"

"And both of us have access to the account?"

"Yes, everything is joint. You and Mr. Straussbecker." Coates grabbed a folder lying beside him. "Now, for people in your position, there are several investment options to discuss."

Joshua rolled his eyes. "I understand your job is to sell, Mr. Coates. But to be frank, I really need to analyze this data. You do have these figures on a computer, don't you?"

"Of course. We printed it out only this morning."

"I mean, the raw data. Something on a USB stick or a hard drive of some sort?"

Coates' eyes glazed over for a moment. Then he realized what Joshua was asking for. "I think one of our technicians can courier over a floppy disk."

A grin spread across Joshua's face. "A floppy disk it shall be. How delightful."

"Takes me a little while to catch on," said Coates. "But someday I would like to learn how to use a computer."

"No problem," said Joshua.

Coates put down his tea and stood up. "Well, I wouldn't want to waste any of your time. I'll leave these brochures."

"Thank you for coming all the way out here," said Axel.

Coates handed the pamphlets to Joshua. "I'd like to let you know more about some opportunities we have in our Savings and Loan subsidiaries-"

"Perhaps in a few weeks," said Axel. "Thank you for coming." Axel grabbed Coates's jacket and showed him out.

By the time he was gone, Joshua had already looked through the printout again. Then took out his iPhone and did some comparing. It was going to be a huge job going through all this data. He could have easily crunched it in Excel, if Coates had just brought a disk with them. If there even existed spreadsheet programs in the 1980s.

After watching Coates drive off, Axel came back to the living room and sat down. "You could have listened to his pitch. We don't want anyone to take a dislike to us."

"Everything's going fine," said Joshua. "You can repay the money tomorrow. But there are some discrepancies between my data and Coates's. Take a look."

Joshua handed Axel the phone and printout.

"Look at today's date on both. The final numbers don't match."

Axel glanced at the phone. "You think there is some sort of fraud occurring on their behalf?"

"No," said Joshua, leaning back on the couch, "it's possible that our investment is affecting the markets in ways we don't-"

Before he finished, the entire room exploded with blue lightening. To Axel it felt like an explosion. Except everything was still there, intact. At first he thought someone was shooting at the house.

Instead it was waves of energy and air, like a storm erupting in the center of his living room.

Everything went dark. Then Axel watched as the bolts of lightening circled Joshua, enveloping him. His body went translucent.

Axel stood up. "Oh my god-"

There was a flash and Joshua disappeared.

45

It was the same collider. Except for all the lattice work. He was in the middle of the gulag.

Joshua looked around.

Something had changed.

Everything was white. Surrounding him was...not a fence, but some sort of net. It was the exact same place where he had disappeared. Yet everything felt strange. He couldn't move. Or maybe he could, but only in a limited arc.

Walking forward was impossible. Like he was in a bubble, preventing him from escaping. As if his legs were bound, except he could turn his head. He saw a console. With monitors and lights.

Behind it stood Axel, the elderly version, and François. They high-fived each other. Joshua tried to moved towards them. With great difficulty he found he could shuffle sideways. A bit. He caught sight of his right hand. It was translucent.

"What is this place?" he shouted.

The older Axel approached. "Don't move. Just stay where you are."

"I can barely hear you." All around the hum of machinery filled the air.

"We have a way of bringing you back."

"But my hand-"

"It's okay," said François. "Finding you was the hard part. We still need to run more tests. You're going to fade back into the past."

"When?"

"In about...thirty-five seconds," said Axel.

For a moment Axel and François stabbed at their consoles, muttering to each other. Joshua saw their displays spit out a range of numbers. Something big was happening. He wasn't sure what it was.

"Joshua," yelled François, "listen. The next window. From your perspective. It will be in twenty-three days. Five in the morning, Chicago time. So make sure you've got pants on, okay?"

Joshua nodded. "Sure, but—"

There was an explosion of air and light. As before, everything went dark. Even the monitors surrounding François and Axel. Blue bolts of lightening filled the tunnel again.

When the disturbance calmed down, the lights came back on.

Joshua was gone.

The older Axel turned to François. "Do you

think he'll make it? You think he'll still be alive by the time the next window opens?"

"I don't know. It's up to luck."

"There's no way to get him back quicker?"

"We're looking for another fissure, but it could take months."

Axel nodded. "Today has been amazing. You've done good work. Hopefully this wasn't random chance."

"I don't know," said François. "This data. It'll take us another week to digest it all." François leaned back in his chair. Everything that had happened was all his fault. He hadn't told Joshua there was only a sixteen percent chance they could get him out of there. At least by giving a time and date, he would know if they'd succeeded or failed. "Let's go back to the lab. We need to process this data."

46

Axel was shaking. He had curled up into a ball when he felt a hand on his shoulder. Turning around, he saw it was Joshua. "How did you come back?"

"I don't know."

"Where have you been?"

"I was in the future."

"Why are you still here?" said Axel, trembling.

"I don't know."

Joshua looked at his hands. "I'm whole again."

Axel shook his head. "I need a drink."

"I could use one too." Joshua sat down, grabbed a cup of tea and sipped it. The liquid tasted real to him. The translucence. The invisible barrier. He hadn't really traveled all the way through time, had he?

"Just halfway there," he muttered. "I think they're trying to get me out of here."

"They?" asked Axel. "Who is they?"

"You, and another colleague."

Axel went quiet, not sure how to deal with the idea that some future version of himself existed. "So...what does that mean? Is there any point in us continuing, on our end?"

"I don't know."

"Maybe we won't need the collider after all," said Axel. "What do you plan to do?"

"I have twenty-three days left in 1987."

Axel picked up a mug of tea. "I think the best thing is to go down to the basement and stay there. Don't go out for the next twenty-three days."

Joshua nodded. "Yeah...probably for the best."

"But first," said Axel, "let's go to the kitchen. And start drinking."

47

The brand of peach schnapps was Gölles. From Austria.

Axel had smuggled it through customs in his luggage since the brand wasn't sold in America. Joshua couldn't help but smile. The Axel he'd known at CERN would never conceive of such behavior.

"But the problem," continued Axel, "is that it is hard to get decent German food around here."

"What are you talking about? All these cities and towns in the Northern Midwest are filled with restaurants that serve German food."

"No, not at all. These people know nothing about German cuisine. Except for Oktoberfest. And then they serve American beer, which is dreadful."

"Yes, well, we agree on that. But in the far future, it's getting better."

"How?"

"Microbrews. From California."

"Like what? Budweiser? Ten different flavors?" said Axel, pouring himself another glass of schnapps. He drank it straight, unlike Joshua, who diluted his drink with soda water. After he finished filling the glass, he added some to Joshua's drink. "It's a pity we won't get to study more of you."

"At least you'll have my math to work on."

"That's what I worry about," said Axel. "I'm hesitant to incorporate it into my work. It might upset the future. Either way...twenty-three days.... It will be so strange to have you ripped away from us."

"Why? Are you going to miss me?"

"I suppose I will. You've opened my eyes to the potential beyond our research."

"Don't forget, this was all because of an accident."

Clomping echoed in from the hallway. Axel's wife, Marianne, a tall blond woman from Bavaria, wandered in with their son, Thomas.

"Say goodnight to your father," said Marianne.

"Can you come and tuck me in, daddy?"

Joshua was surprised to hear the child had already picked up an American accent. He couldn't be more than five or six. Then grimaced when he thought about what lie ahead for the boy.

Axel stood up, lifting his son up into his arms. "There we go." He turned to Joshua. "I'll be back in a minute. Duty calls."

Joshua slugged back his drink. He had given a lot of thought to what he was going to say to Axel about his family. About the future. He'd been debating it in his own mind. Maybe he didn't have to say something directly.

In the empty kitchen, he stood up and wandered around. Found the phone book. Just below the ancient microwave oven, the one with dials. He opened up the big thick yellow pages for the Chicago area.

Flicked through until he arrived at 'Travel Agencies.'

48

Joshua heard Axel walking toward the kitchen.

"They say it's awful having children," said Axel. "Like it's the end of our lives as physicists. We never recover from having satisfied our wives. The best scientists are always the ones who aren't married. All that extra energy and time to do math." As Axel entered the kitchen he saw Joshua put down the receiver of the old rotary phone. "Who was that?"

"Pizza. I hope you like anchovies."

"Always." Axel grabbed the bottle and refreshed their drinks. "It's best to be careful. You don't want to do too much stuff. Have too much contact with people. I don't want to see you get hit by a bus."

Joshua sat down. "I doubt that's going to happen."

Axel examined the near empty liquor bottle. "Good thing I have another liter of the raspberry kind behind the spaghetti sauce."

Joshua took a long sip from his glass. "I think we should talk."

"Don't use that tone with me." Axel shook his head and poured himself a double. "I don't want to hear about the future."

"This is important."

"I don't want to hear it. I don't need to know that I might lose my legs in a bus crash, or something like that."

"What if it was about your son?"

49

Axel awoke to the aroma of bacon permeating the upstairs bedroom. Marianne had her routine for dealing with his occasional hangover. She was well acquainted with the German propensity to overdo it when it came to alcohol. His body felt like lead, and his stomach felt like molten lead. Rumblings of nausea arose as he put on his bathrobe and trudged down the stairs. His son was probably already up and off playing with friends. Wouldn't see his father sleeping in on a Sunday morning. At least Axel didn't have any classes to teach today.

He wandered into the kitchen. Bacon was indeed cooking on the stove, with eggs and some kind of seasoned potatoes. He grabbed a drink of water from the sink.

Marianne appeared in the doorway to the basement, where they kept a small laundry room.

He sat down at the kitchen table. Looked at the clock. It said eleven-thirty. Glanced at the morning paper. Since they'd moved from Germany five years ago, Axel had yet to understand the American obsession with boxing and baseball. He missed all the soccer news that filled up European sports sections. Americans would never be into it, would they?

"Coffee?" asked Marianne.

"Sure."

She poured him a cup and brought it over to the table. "You went hard last night," she said in German.

"Yeah."

"Joshua didn't have any breakfast."

Axel was alarmed. "He's already up?"

"Yes. He left the house two hours ago. Went to visit his father who lives in Washington."

Axel stood up straight. His entire body electrified. "Oh my god...."

50

MacLean was already five minutes late. His driver had already phoned up from the front lobby. Hell, he was lucky to have his own private ride. One of the concessions to someone of his stature working for the CIA. Which made most of the other civilian staffers angry. They had to find their own way to meetings in Washington. What they didn't know was that the real reason for the chauffeur was because MacLean had a terrible record for arriving on time. It had annoyed his superiors when stationed in Bonn. So someone had granted him the use of a car and driver. Once granted, privileges amongst Army officers were hard to rescind.

Nevertheless, he was running late.

Too many reports had come in from Afghanistan. The ISI question had once again fallen into his lap, despite the fact he was no longer dispatched to Germany.

Just when he had gathered all the notes for his presentation at the White House, and was about to leave, Raven appeared in the doorway. Blocking his way.

"Guess what?"

"Don't have time. I have a meeting with the DCI in twenty-five minutes."

"Our stock market Einstein. I finally got something out of my NSA contacts."

MacLean's glance narrowed. "You must be pretty good to get one of them in bed."

Raven rolled her eyes. "If you think-" she began, anger rising inside of her.

"I don't." MacLean pushed her out of his way. "Tell me what happens next."

She followed him out to the elevators. "Well, the guys over there have nothing before six weeks ago."

"Really? What is he? A Ruskie?"

"We have a voice recording of him. Sounds American."

"Could be from Canada."

"We checked. No dice."

"That's weird."

"He's on a flight right now. Lands at National in two hours."

MacLean dropped one of his files just as the elevator arrived. Fortunately it was almost empty.

"What do you want me to do? You're the secret agent."

"I need approval for-"

MacLean hopped on the elevator. "Yeah, yeah. Whatever. I've got to go."

Raven smiled as the doors closed. MacLean was obviously a hands-off kind of guy.

51

Washington was in the middle of a crack epidemic.

Twelve blocks from the White House you might end up getting shot. In fact, the president did exactly that, in 1981.

That's what people didn't understand about the city. Most who worked there, usually for the federal government, lived somewhere else. Lots of people lived on the other side of the river, in the sprawling Virginia suburbs that lined the I-95 corridor. Or they bought houses, as Joshua's parents had, in one of the nicer suburbs just north of the city.

Chevy Chase was the name of the town where he'd grown up. It was a lovely, upper-middle class area. Filled with colonial-style houses. Lining well-kept streets dotted with foliage and old-growth trees. A complete contrast to northeast Washington. Even places like Foggy Bottom and Dupont Circle-they were still pretty dangerous to be walking around after midnight. Although, in thirty years they'd changed quite a bit. There was still the underlying grit, even today.

One of Joshua's friends had been shot walking home from a bar at two in the morning. Not because the guy resisted the assailant, just because he happened to be in the wrong place at the wrong time. Someone who'd grown up in Joshua's old neighborhood. A guy who'd moved with the rest of his friends downtown. He'd taken a short cut down a dark street. Once the thief had gotten his wallet, he'd fired a bullet right into his friend's stomach. His friend didn't even know he was injured until he arrived at a pizza place around the corner, trailing blood. And a girl waiting at the counter screamed. Most people didn't understand. Sometimes when you got shot, you didn't even notice it, if it didn't hit an area with a bundle of nerves. You could walk just fine. Once his friend had sat down, he'd immediately passed out. And woke up two days later in the hospital. Lucky that he wasn't paralyzed.

The first thing Joshua had done upon arrival was taken the subway out to Chevy Chase. From there, just in case there was someone who was surveilling him, he decided to take a cab. As they drove along, Joshua couldn't believe he was sitting in an almost brand new Caprice Classic.

They pulled up to a large two-story colonial-style house. Which his father had bought before he was born. Still quite a few mortgage payments before it was paid off.

The back door of the cab swung open and Joshua emerged, wallet in hand. "Hey, look, I'm going to be here for a few minutes. You'll stick around?"

"Well, I don't know-" said the driver.

Joshua handed him a twenty. "This'll keep you covered for now."

The cabbie smiled and nodded in acknowledgment.

Joshua wandered up the front walk. Looked up at the large house ahead of him. Was it really a good idea to do this? He hesitated, and looked at his watch. It was three-thirty on a Sunday afternoon. He approached the front door. Made sure his necktie was tied tight.

He rang the doorbell, then brushed his hair nervously.

The door opened revealing Joshua's mother. She was, as he could never remember her, a slim woman in her mid-thirties. "Hello," she said. "Can I help you?"

Joshua cleared his throat. "Yes, ma'am. My name is Jason Saunders from the State Department. I'm the executive assistant to Michael Adams." That sounded right, he thought. That was the name of the guy his father had always talked about. His boss. "I'm terribly sorry to bother your husband on his day off-"

"No, it's no problem. Do you have any ID?"

Joshua was prepared for this. "This is kind of embarrassing, but I left the office in such a hurry I forgot it at my desk."

221

"And you had to come in person?"

Joshua's eyes darted around for a moment. "Uh, yeah, those were my orders."

His mother frowned. She knew what kind of work her husband was in. This might mean he'd be on a plane by the end of the day. "Well," she said, looking him over, "you better come in."

52

As Joshua waited in the foyer, his eyes lingered on the wallpaper.

He remembered it from his childhood, the powder blue flowers on strips of alternating white and gold.

How he'd hated it.

On a rack nearby he spotted the green raincoat he'd worn as a child. A flood of emotion came over him. He felt tears welling, but he held back. This was the life he used to live, wasn't it?

He heard the familiar bips and beeps of an old Nintendo game being played on the television. Super Mario Brothers. The original game. That was it.

He walked further into the house.

In the living room doorway he looked to his right and saw an old-style Panasonic TV, all wood paneling and grey metal.

His seven-year-old self, sitting on the carpet. Tapping on the buttons of a controller.

His seven-year-old self.

He remembered playing this game in this same room. But he didn't remember this actual day. Had it happened?

Joshua sat down next to the boy. He looked at the screen. "Having trouble?"

"It's world eight-three," said his younger self. "I can't get past this gap."

"Here-let me see." He took the controller from his younger self. Made the jump.

"You're pretty good at this."

Joshua smiled. "I've had lots of practice."

53

Adam Sinclair wasn't one to suffer fools. And that's what he saw lurking in his living room. "Why is he here?" he whispered to his wife. "There's no reason someone would come to my house without contacting me first. Not on a day off."

"What did you want me to do?" asked Joshua's mother. "He was right there. And he sounded sincere. He's wearing a suit. Don't tell me Soviet agents would show up at our house...."

"You have no idea who this person is. And I've never seen him before."

Adam flexed his left triceps. He was a slab of meat of a human being. Many a morning had been spent in the gym before work. Making sure he wouldn't be taken down on one of his foreign trips abroad. He'd already been to Nigeria and Oman this year. And, off the record, he'd also been to Nicaragua.

But that was a secret, even to his wife and most of the people at the office.

The living room was divided from the kitchen and dining room by a set of French doors.

Adam Sinclair observed the older Joshua. "And he says he's from State?"

"He seems harmless enough."

"We'll see about that. I'm going to give Rogerson a call. And I need to get my sidearm from the upstairs closet."

"Adam-"

"Just keep an eye on them." A million thoughts raced through Adam Sinclair's mind as he climbed the rear staircase. Anyone from the office could have called him. Or even sent a message via the new fax machine he had installed in his basement office.

No, this didn't make any sense at all.

He had to get this guy out of the house as quickly as possible.

54

The white camper van worked well on streets like this.

Old avenues with plenty of cars parked on the sides of the street. The van could park without making waves. Cars were pulling in and out all day long. The camper only became a problem in the far suburbs. Near houses with generous lawns. Where any unusual vehicle stood out.

In locations like those, surveillance became a far greater hassle.

So for Raven, and her two associates in the back of the van, they knew they'd gotten a lucky break. It hadn't been easy tracking him down. It was only when he made a transaction at a bank in Chevy Chase that they'd caught him. He'd spent more than an hour there, dealing with bankers. Then they had to follow him in the taxi.

The audio guy pointed his high frequency shotgun microphone at the house. It picked up sounds through even the thickest concrete.

This was the first time Raven had coordinated her surveillance with a cellular telephone. The thing was bulky, hardly the kind of device you could take on the run with you. It weighed as much as a brick. But it kept her in touch with headquarters, without the need of a radio mast, which was good.

And it cut down the cost. In the old days they would have needed three vehicles. With the cellular phone they could get away with one to follow the mark.

Roger, the audio guy, listened carefully on giant headphones, plugged into a complicated-looking mixing board and a reel-to-reel recorder. With one hand on a remote control for the microphone stand that allowed it to move three hundred and sixty degrees from its position under a frosted dome atop the roof.

Meanwhile the photographer, Denny, stood by the window. Three different tripods set up with cameras, each with a different telephoto lens. All synced together.

Raven was on the phone with Langley. "Yeah, that's right," she said. "Thirty-six thirty Pollard.... Yeah, in Bethesda.... Of course I'm sure, we're across the street..."

There was a long pause, as she waited for them to check the address.

Her eyes widened.

"Seriously? Okay...." She nodded into the phone. "Yeah, we'll be careful...okay, bye."

She hung up. Turned to Roger and Denny. "You won't believe this. Einstein here just popped in to visit one of ours. Do we have anything on audio?"

Roger shook his head. "I've got a kid playing video games. That useful to you?"

Raven opened one of the cupboards above Roger's head. "Do we have any guns?"

Both men gave her a what-the-fuck-have-you-gotten-us-into look. They weren't the type of guys who went into combat.

"Just in case."

55

Adam kept silent as he strapped on his policeman's holster. Then put the navy sports jacket over it. He had every intention of making sure this guy knew who the boss of the situation was.

He had just hung up the phone with the lone secretary on duty at the state department. No one had been in at his office all day. One moment after he disconnected the line, Adam decided it might have been a mistake not asking the secretary to call the police.

Probably for the better. His wife knew their address. The secretary would have to find it in the top secret directory. That would take time. And the situation had yet to warrant such action. He reminded himself that the key action in any hostage situation was to keep the opposition talking. Then at least they won't do anything crazy.

Adam headed back down the rear staircase where his wife was still keeping watch in the kitchen.

"Get Josh out of there and call the cops, okay? Nobody at State sent anyone."

"Why didn't you tell them to send the police?"

"Don't argue, just get him upstairs, now."

56

Joshua stroked his younger self's hair. God. Had he ever been this young? He retracted his hand.

The scene didn't look good. Not for a man his age. He turned back to the TV.

"See. Now world eight—four is really easy. You just have to get to Bowser and you'll be fine."

"Really?" said the boy. "But the world before was so hard—"

"Trust me. You have nothing to worry about after that. In fact, I bet if they made a sequel to this game, it'd be way easier."

"You think so?"

"Yup. There're kids across America, just like you."

"Josh," screamed their mother from across the hall, "it's time for your bath."

The boy shook his head. "But it's only two thirty—"

His mother walked into the room. "Now, mister."

She reached over and dragged him to his feet. The boy pushed the pause button on the video game console. "I don't want to—"

"Quit the whining and move."

She marched the boy out of the room. "We don't have to do it right now..."

"Yes, we do."

Joshua knew better. He could see the subtle look of panic on her face. Turning around, he looked over at the video game on the TV. He switched it off.

"I see you've met my son."

Joshua whipped around.

His father stood in front of the French doors.

How does one respond to a remark like that? he wondered. For the first time in over fifteen years, he saw his long—dead father. His hair is so much darker, he thought. He's even a little bit skinnier.

Joshua felt an overwhelming sense of pain and fear and agony. Tears welled in his eyes. "I'm sorry—" he said.

Adam Sinclair was having none of it. This guy was clearly a nutcase. He looked like he was about to cry. "I don't think you understand the thin ice you're on, mister."

Joshua walked up closer to his father.

Adam Sinclair moved his hand over his holster. "Impersonating a federal official—"

234

Joshua hugged him tightly.

Adam didn't know what to do. The man was obviously disturbed.

Reluctantly he embraced Joshua.

57

Inside the camper, it was getting warmer. The air conditioning had been switched off as to not interfere with the microphone. It was one of those odd days in November where usually you'd be thankful for the warmth.

Raven had no plans to stick around. Except that Denny, the photographer, had yet to get a decent shot of the guy's face.

Roger, the audio guy, turned to her. "The mother just phoned nine—one—one."

"Shit." Raven thought about the implications of remaining there.

They might be complicit. Observing a crime taking place. The CIA wasn't supposed to be doing domestic surveillance. Raven's people were all local private investigators. From a legal perspective, they'd be up shit creek. Even if their target wasn't a confirmed American citizen. She'd only gone this far because she knew MacLean didn't care. As long as they maintained a low profile.

And to think she was doing this for him as a favor. This was the FBI's turf.

Raven turned around. "This is getting messy." She looked over at Denny. "Once we've got his photo let's get out of here." Then crouched down beside Roger. "What else are you hearing?"

"I don't know—it sounds like the guy's pleading or something—"

58

Adam Sinclair was in a panic.

He strained every fiber in his physical body to keep from showing it. It was clear that a mentally ill man had come to visit. Was it only a matter of time before he tried to attack? The guy was probably schizophrenic. Or confused. Gently Adam pushed him away. Slowly started to walk backwards.

"Listen—"

Joshua moved away from him and wiped his eyes. "This is very hard for me to explain. Something very bad is going to happen."

There was an awkward pause.

"Why did you come to my house?"

Joshua shook his head. "You're not understanding me."

Adam looked at him in confusion. "What is there to understand?"

His first instinct was to tackle this guy. Escalating the conversation to violence was probably not a good idea. Instead Adam backed off and glanced at his wife in the kitchen. She was on the phone.

Joshua leaned over to get the same view. He realized what was happening. "Wait," he said. "Don't call the police."

He raised both of his arms up, like he was surrendering. "Don't you see—"

He thought about it for a minute. This was it. The moment he put all of his cards on the table. "I'm your son. I've come to you from the future."

Adam Sinclair backed off and drew his pistol. With one smooth precise motion. Undid the safety catch. Held it with both hands pointing at Joshua. He would shoot him first in the shoulder. If that didn't stop him, he'd aim for the thigh.

"What I want you to do is listen to me very carefully. I want you to calmly sit down on that sofa. In a few minutes some officers will arrive. They'll want to take you in for assessment."

"You're not listening. I'm not a crazy person. I know it sounds that way but I want you to listen."

"You need to sit down."

"I want you to listen to me for thirty seconds, then I'll walk out that door and you'll never see me again." Joshua looked at his father's face. He wasn't buying it. "In your line of work the last thing you want is the cops coming to your house. Am I right?"

"Yeah."

"And if you discharge that weapon, and one of your bullets hits me, that'll mean career suicide. Right?"

Adam Sinclair stared at his son coldly. "You've got thirty seconds."

59

Roger took off his headphones. Looked over at Raven. "You've got to hear this yarn he's spinning."

She grabbed the headset. But all she heard was Joshua saying goodbye. "Dammit. He's leaving. Get ready for his exit."

The photographer began snapping away. He took four photos as the door opened. He had to be careful. There were only seventeen exposures left on each roll of film. Using the remote follow focus and exposure timer, he snapped away. All three cameras in sync. Holding the largest telephoto lens tightly.

As the shutters clicked away, Joshua exited his parents house. And ran for the taxi. He got in the back and the cab screeched off.

"Whoever this guy is," said Denny, "he sure knows how to evade the prying eyes."

"Come on," said Raven, grabbing Roger. "Let's get a move on." She turned to Denny. "Did you get a clear shot of him?"

"Not really."

"Reload your cameras. We'll try to get you another chance."

60

"And everyone agrees that he knew what he was doing?"

"That's the consensus," said Raven.

She was standing in front of MacLean's desk. As he examined a blue file folder. It was now eight o'clock at night. Raven had familial obligations. She didn't want to be here. MacLean didn't seem much happier to be working late. He'd had a rough day. Continuous meetings since lunch.

MacLean closed the folder. His brain was struggling to keep up with the facts. "Run it through one more time what happened."

"We tailed him through Chevy Chase, but then we got stuck in traffic. We managed to get a hold of the cab driver before he left the area, but he only confirmed our guy got off at the subway."

"So he isn't stupid. Maybe he's been trained for some kind of operation."

"By the Soviets?"

"I don't know. I looked at the police report. Both Sinclair and his wife say the incident was little more than an overzealous vacuum salesman. The guy got Sinclair's name from some kind of government list."

"If you believe that—"

"I don't. That's why I want you to step things up."

Raven looked at him cautiously. "Are you sure you want to wear this? Our jurisdiction—"

"I don't give a damn." MacLean adjusted his uniform. "Something smells here. Besides, if we hand this over to another agency, I'm certain we'll never track this guy again. Finding him the first time was sheer luck. He won't put himself out in the open again. Not after today. We'll never catch up to him until the crime has already been committed. Whoever he represents is important. With some serious money behind them. We can't take this lightly. We know he's not an American citizen, don't we?"

"Yeah, we're pretty sure."

"Pretty sure?"

"Almost a hundred percent."

"So it's likely he'll try and leave the country."

"At some point."

"In which case, it will fall into our jurisdiction. There's no point in going over all the bureaucratic nonsense."

"But—"

"We'll just invoke national security. If worse comes to worse."

Raven looked at her watch. "I think you're up shit creek without a paddle. And you're desperately trying to justify being there before your canoe overturns."

MacLean smiled. "You might be right." He twisted one of his cufflinks. "But after your last incident, I'm sure this is something you'd like to sink your teeth into."

Raven felt exhausted. "Fine. But you're asking me to look for this guy in a city of three million people." She began to pace. "How? He could be anywhere."

MacLean thought about it. "We have that new computerized tracking of hotel bookings. See if you can cross reference it with his flight times."

"But there are hundreds of hotels in Washington. Which one would he go to?"

61

The Watergate Hotel complex had some of the tallest buildings in Foggy Bottom.

But not many Americans knew that.

While the complex was synonymous with Richard Nixon's presidency, few people understood how vast it was. Five large buildings on the banks of the Potomac River. All designed by an Italian architect in a gesture of looking towards the future. A supposed compliment to a never—built freeway at the base of the structure.

The tallest of the buildings was only about fifteen stories tall. And even that had been a fight. A building of such Modernist design had clashed with the citizenry of Washington that cherished more conservative architectural aesthetics. The city's founding fathers, whose legacy was carried on by federal government bureaucrats, had ensured that no structure would run higher than the dome of the Capitol Building. Add to that the fact that Modernist building design was considered incredibly radical in the mid—20th century. Especially in a city that prided itself on its Colonial—era roots.

Hell, even the Protestants had taken up the charge once they discovered the complex was to be partially financed by the Vatican.

One of the good things, however, was that when one checked into the hotel, the security system was so state—of—the—art that no unwanted visitors could access the grounds of the five different buildings without going undetected. But because of the way the complex was designed, it was ideal for surveillance. After days of searching, Raven had finally hit the jackpot and found their target. Extremely lucky that he was still in the area. She had guessed that an individual of immense resources would want to stay somewhere nice. So the team had scoured the top hotels in the city first.

The guy had checked in for five nights so far. Exactly the kind of thing that made you stand out in the hotel staff's minds. Maybe he wasn't the professional they'd thought he was.

One of the hotel clerks was an informant for the CIA.

They'd found a reason to move the guy to a different room while he was out. To the other side of the building. Facing the south courtyard. Across from where the CIA had a surveillance post set up. They had a perfect line—of—sight view of the man they now knew was Joshua Sinclair.

Raven sat at the desk, watching the surveillance guys do their work. With a note pad and pen. If Sinclair left the hotel, she would pursue.

"So," said Roger, "all this guy is doing is watching TV and cracking open beer. How long is this going to take? I've got Frank Stallone tickets for tonight."

Raven smiled. "Well, I wouldn't want Frank to play to an empty room."

"Hardy—har—har."

She had to agree, though, surveillance was not a family man's game. Or a family woman's.

This was actually a pretty luxurious set—up. She had heard of situations, years ago, where a couple guys in Europe had been placed in a church attic. For weeks on end. Unable to leave. Those same guys had surveiled a country house in South Africa. They'd had to dig a trench and put a wire fence up to keep the lions and tigers out. At least Raven and the boys had a working bathroom. Better than most stakeouts.

"Be glad you don't have children to take care of," she said to Roger.

Denny, the photographer looked over. "My kids have given up on me tucking them into bed."

"I know the feeling."

Raven started to pace. "We've been here for two nights. This isn't working. We need to draw him out."

Denny smiled. "We could send up a hooker. I'd love to get a few extra shots for my private collection."

251

Raven almost slapped him. But then a smile came across her face. "That's not a bad idea."

"Well, if you're paying..."

Raven picked up the room phone and dialed a number.

"Hey, Vicki, it's Raves. I have something for you to do tonight.... And if you could give Samantha a call too, that would be great."

62

Few things had disappointed Joshua more than the entertainment options available in 1987. He never remembered it being this bad. But apparently it was.

Joshua lay on his bed. For the past six days he'd placed the 'do not disturb' sign on his door. He'd been getting most of his nourishment through room service. Now he worried all the rich foods were affecting his mind. He hadn't risked being seen again by anyone in that household. Or by any police that might be looking for him.

But there was the problem that he'd made himself known to the authorities of this time period. It had been a mistake. What was he going to do here? He wanted to make contact with some people at the CIA. But not yet. Joshua had phoned Axel to tell him where he was. But the truth was Joshua was now out of Axel's care, as it were. Still, after telling his father about the future, it felt like a great burden had been lifted off him.

At least he'd done what he could.

Maybe.

Assuming his father believed him.

Two days after visiting his family, Joshua had planned to go to George Washington University. To look up some old colleagues. Convince them to change their support for militias in Afghanistan.

But he'd been stopped by the police. Shown them the fake ID Axel had procured for him. After that he realized how vulnerable he was. He'd gone back to the hotel and stayed there.

He'd amused himself with the cable box. Ancient movies and even more dated pornography. He'd paid a visit to a bookstore. But mostly he just waited. And drank. Tonight he'd ordered a steak and french fries from the kitchen. Washed it down with an overpriced and under—sized bottle of Beaujolais. Now he sipped the last of the wine, while watching the end of the Sonny and Cher Reunion Special.

Had the 80s really been this lame?

He reached for the remote control and flicked through the other stations. Twenty channels. They only have twenty channels. He found a station where "Miami Vice" was just about to start.

Maybe if he wore sunglasses he could leave the hotel. Not be noticed in the street.

Before being stopped by the cops, he'd spent a couple of hours walking around Washington. Everything was a little bit different. The stores were somewhat the same, but the displays were old. And the food...everything was so...white bread. Just a lot of bland stuff. And Washington felt so much more dangerous than he'd remembered.

There were so many more crazy people in the past. Had things really been this bad?

On his first night, Joshua had gone out onto his hotel room balcony. Listened to the sounds of the night. Twice he'd heard gunshots. Something that didn't happen in the Washington of the future. Which, in a way, gave Joshua some hope. Life was getting better. Even if television news convinced the population it was getting worse. So many people had waxed nostalgic about the 1980s over the last fifteen years. But in truth it was all a bit depressing. He had to admit, though, the punks did have an interesting sense of fashion.

The rotary phone on the bedside table rang.

"Uh, hello? Yeah...really...? Under my door? ...thanks.... Bye." He hung up and got out of bed. Walked over to the door. Joshua picked up a piece of paper that had been slid into the room. It was a coupon. For free booze.

Now he had an excuse to leave.

63

The bar turned out to be lonelier than Joshua was.

It was down on the second floor of the building. Just across the hall from the restaurant. Not far past the entrance was a piano that looked like it was seldom played. The room was nice. Wood paneling. Low lit lights. High backed dark leather chairs. A bar well stocked with expensive whiskeys. In front of which stood a bartender in a black vest and bowtie.

At a far table in the corner he saw two obese businessmen. A lone elderly man in a suit occupied the bar. Seated below an ancient television. Although Joshua figured it was probably brand new at this point in time. It played a basketball game. Just started.

This place must do big business during the holiday season. But right now Thanksgiving was still weeks away.

And to think it was a Friday night.

Joshua approached the bar. "Hey, they slid this coupon for a couple of free drinks under my door." He laid down the piece of paper.

"What'll it be?" said the bartender. The man had a rough, weathered look to his face. Like a cowboy. Or a crack addict. Despite the bow tie and the suspenders. His mustache gave away a certain working class vibe. As if, in a previous life, he'd been an alcoholic cop who had taken things too far.

Joshua thought about what he wanted to drink. He looked over the bottles behind the bar. At least hard liquor hadn't changed much in the past. "Give me a whiskey sour."

With nothing else to do, the bartender, seemingly disinterested in conversation, left Joshua alone with his drink. The elderly man ordered another martini with grammar so imprecise Joshua suspected he didn't speak English. So he turned his attentions to the TV. Spent the next hour watching the New York Knicks get pounded by the Washington Bullets.

"After tonight I think the Knicks will believe in Friday the thirteenth, don't you think so Bob?" said the announcer just before Joshua ordered his third drink.

As the commercial came on, Joshua stared at his empty glass. Thinking about his next move. He had to leave the hotel room. The smart move would be to stay there until François rescued him. But he needed to take action.

In less than 18 days he would be gone.

His thoughts were interrupted by the chatter of a bunch of drunk girls.

Joshua looked over. Hmm. Three cuties. A black girl. An Asian girl. And a Nordic blond. He hadn't felt this excited since he visited Hamburg a couple of years ago. The girl version of a candy store.

All three wore white bridesmaid's dresses. It sounded like the party had been going on for a while.

"And Jessie's nephew was adorable," said the black girl.

"A six year old in a tuxedo!" said the Asian girl.

"Can you imagine?" said the blond girl. "The money Bobby and Cindy must have thrown down on that!"

"No, you don't understand," said the black girl, "Jessie's marrying up."

"Yeah, girl," said the Nordic blond, "it ain't just the ladies digging for gold these days."

Joshua turned back to the TV.

Part of him wanted to rush over to them. The girls must be in a hooking up mood. He hadn't had any female companionship In a great long time. Then again, it might be girl's night out. Maybe they wanted to do their own thing.

"Bartender, another sour, please."

64

It was now or never.

How come he was still shy approaching women, even in his thirties? Maybe shyness was something you didn't outgrow. Especially when it came to hitting on women in a bar.

Joshua stared up at the TV. Ten minutes to go and it was a lost cause for the Knicks. A commercial break came on for Pabst Blue Ribbon.

Once again he stared at his drink, only to hear more giggling behind him. Something told him he could not let this slide.

Joshua turned back to peek at the girls. A table of hotties. The black girl gave him a long, drawn—out gaze. He couldn't let her get away with that, could he? He stood up, stabilized himself on the bar stool, and ambled over to the girls.

"Ladies," he said, almost falling over himself he was so drunk, "my apologies to interrupt your conversation, but I was wondering if I could ask you all a question?"

"Go ahead," said the blond.

"What kind of girl gets married on Friday the thirteenth?"

The entire table burst out laughing.

"A girl," said Raven, "with wealthy cheapskate parents. That's who."

Joshua swayed a bit. He leaned on the table's only empty chair.

The Asian girl looked up at him. "What brings you here on a Friday night?"

"You don't want to know."

"Come on, tell us," said the blond.

Joshua shook his head. "It's really complicated and I've had a rough day. The hotel moved my room, and—"

"What are you?" said Raven. "A hit man?"

"No. Of course not. I'm an engineering physicist."

Oohs and aahs came from the girls.

"A brainiac!" said the Asian.

"Not quite. I'm thirty—five and I'm still not married."

More aahs.

Joshua began to sway some more.

"You can sit down, you know," said the blond girl.

"No, there's no way I'm sitting down with three girls who went to a cursed wedding. I've got to get back to the game. No way."

65

Samantha, who Joshua had learned was the name of the blond, and Vicki, who was the Asian girl, had started to drift off.

Not that Joshua would have noticed...

—unlike Raven, who was hanging on every word of Joshua's.

He had spent the last forty—five minutes explaining the finer points of sub—atomic particle measurement. "So you see, the Planck length is a number to the minus thirty—five. Nothing smaller can exist. At that size everything breaks down into vibrating strings of spacetime. But I've gone even smaller. That's how I got here."

"Really?" said Raven. "I arrived by taxi."

Joshua laughed. Talking about theoretical physics made him excited. And he seemed to be metabolizing the alcohol quicker. He felt more sober, more alert than before.

Raven rubbed his arm. "That's amazing that you know so much."

The bartender approached. They were the last people left in the place. The TV was off. "I'm afraid it's last call," he said.

Vicki and Samantha stirred.

"We've got to get to bed," said Vicki.

They both stood up, forking over some cash.

"That should cover it," said Samantha. "We'll see you tomorrow at checkout."

Joshua was surprised they just left Raven with him.

"Night."

And they were gone.

Wow. Girls in the past were more forthcoming than he thought.

Joshua gazed into her eyes. "So your name is Raven. That sounds mysterious."

"You look like a man who could use another drink."

Joshua smiled. He looked down at the empty glasses filling the table. They'd been going pretty hard. "Why don't we do our friend here a favor and head up to the bar? So he can clear off the table."

They found two adjacent high backed stools as the bartender put two whiskey sours down in front of Joshua and Raven.

"Cheers."

"Cheers."

They clinked glasses and took a sip.

264

Joshua moved in closer and took her hand. Her skin was smooth and warm. "What do you want from me? Be honest."

"What do you mean?"

"Whatever it is, you won't get it." Joshua moved in closer and nuzzled her breasts. Then let go of her hand and moved a few inches away.

After a moment she moved over and nuzzled up to him. "What makes you so sure of that? Today's my lucky day."

Her hand reached over for his. He slapped her away.

"No way. Not a chance."

66

Raven belted out an ecstatic scream. In the darkness.

Joshua's hands retracted from her neither regions and she collapsed into his arms. They stayed that way for a few moments. Then kissed some more. And fumbled around in the sheets. Raven fell back, sleepy. Joshua got up and went to the washroom.

Ravens eyes fluttered wide open. Her exhaustion was a ruse.

In the light streaming into the bathroom, she did a quick survey of the room. Nothing special in the drawers, or on the night stand.

But on the desk, next to the television. She found his iPhone, charging. She disconnected it from the power cord.

She tried to turn it on, but couldn't find the switch. Examining it, she stroked the metal contours. Plastic, glass and metal, all smoothly integrated. She'd never seen anything like it before.

"Do you like my telephone?"

Raven crawled back into bed. Caught red handed. "I've never, uh, seen this in any store."

Joshua got into bed and tried to grab the phone from her. She playfully resisted until he gave up.

"I want to see it."

"No, you can't.... It's a secret."

Joshua buried his head in the pillows.

"Who do you call with it?"

He looked up from the pillow. "Right now, nobody. I don't use the phone that much anyway."

"Why not?"

"Well, I'm from the future, so there's no cell phone network around here that works with it. Not yet, anyway."

"Ah," Raven said nonchalantly. She looked back down at the phone. "There's no keypad."

"You have to turn it on."

"So if you don't use the telephone, how do you get a hold of people?"

"I use Skype and Facebook. And LINE. It's cheaper."

"You don't have telephones in the future?"

"We do, but it's different."

"How do you mean?"

"It's just...different. Everyone still has one. Especially at work. And most houses still have them, especially old people. But...you know. I only use mine to order pizza. I guess it depends on your job. Some people prefer to use email."

"What?"

"Electronic mail."

"Uh—huh. How do I turn this on?"

"Press the button on the top."

She did. The iPhone login screen came up. "What's the password?"

Joshua rolled onto his side. "Very funny. See you in the morning."

67

Joshua felt well rested. Maybe too well rested. He had planned to be up by eight o'clock. Get some breakfast to ward off the hangover. Hopefully make a visit to the Georgetown University campus. He knew some people, just like Axel, who might be working there. And perhaps could get him access to the CIA.

For the first time in a while, he had a plan in mind.

Rubbing his eyes, he realized he was still a bit drunk. A bright sliver of sunlight shone in through the window. He stood up and rolled out of bed, still naked. Threw open the curtains.

Out the window he had a perfect view of the courtyard between the buildings. No one was in the pool today. Not in this weather. To his right he watched the sun gleam off the Potomac River. And the forests of Virginia beyond. Stretching out to the horizon. He turned around. And realized Raven was gone. Not good.

For a moment he stood there, his head pounding.

God, the hangover.

And the sunlight.

They should have ordered food before he fell asleep. Something to soak up the alcohol. Even pizza would have been okay. Joshua found some underwear and put them on. He looked over at the desk.

The phone.

The smartphone was gone.

God dammit.

He looked over at the clock. Twelve noon. No one from the hotel had bothered to wake him up. Hadn't the maid staff wanted to come in?

He walked over to the door. Opened it. The 'Do Not Disturb' sign was hanging on the doorknob.

Great. Who knows when Raven had left. It could have been hours ago. Shutting the door, he went back and ripped the sheets off. Searched under the bed. Checked every drawer. There was no sign of the phone anywhere. Something caught his attention from under the desk.

The power cord was still attached to the adapter. He pulled it out. Looked at it. And smiled.

Raven was completely clueless.

The phone was useless enough without the internet. Say they did actually crack the passcode. What would they do with it? Play solitaire? Check his emails? The battery would be dead in less than a day.

Not knowing what else to do, Joshua ordered lunch from room service. Then phoned Axel in

Chicago. Washington was more trouble than it was worth. Maybe he should just let things happen as they were meant to be. Losing his telephone—god only knows how that would affect the future.

Joshua thought about it. Knowing the bureaucracy, they'd investigate until it became too labor intensive. Then file the device away.

Whatever plans he had, they were just too risky. He had to go underground. Just wait it out.

He reached over and dialed the number for Axel's house. Marianne informed him Axel was at work today.

Unusual for a Saturday.

Joshua phoned Axel's lab. The call went direct to his office.

"Hello?" In Chicago Axel looked around his narrow office. He kept his eyes on a visitor seated across from his desk observing his phone call. They'd been talking for well over an hour and a half. The man had come alone. Axel had also arrived at a dead end. With the mathematics of time travel.

"Yes," said Axel into the receiver. "I agree. The smartest course of action is for you to come back here." He grabbed a piece of paper and a pen. "Tell me the flight number.... Call me as soon as you've bought the ticket.... Okay.... Great. Bye."

He hung up. He looked at his visitor. "Well, looks like you're getting everything you wanted."

Sitting across the desk from Axel was Major MacLean.

273

68

The flight back to Chicago had been nice. Flight attendants were much, much friendlier in the 1980s. After they landed at Midway, he'd grabbed his carryon backpack and taken a cab downtown. Since it was Sunday, the University of Chicago campus was mostly deserted. Leaves had changed colors completely. The air was tinged with a cold wind that foreshadowed the Chicago winter. He got the cab driver to drop him off at the large grass median on Midway Plaisance. It gave him a good ten minute walk to think about what he was going to say to Axel.

The question remained: what could he do?

Should he give Axel any hint of what would happen in the future?

Would it really matter? Maybe it was best just to hang out in the past. Like it was a vacation. Yeah. That's what he'd do. Take it easy.

The front door to the physics building was unlocked. Joshua took the stairs to the fourth floor. More delaying. The outer office of the physics department was deserted. No secretary today. And no grad students about. The door to Axel's office was open, just slightly. He knocked and heard a muffled "Come In".

Joshua only got the door halfway open when he froze.

MacLean was sitting behind Axel's desk. The man from CNN.

"Come in. Don't be shy."

Joshua approached slowly. This wasn't good. His mind flashed with images of being hooded like he was a prisoner in Iraq.

"Please," gestured MacLean, "sit down."

There was an awkward silence as they looked each other over. Like dogs preparing for a fight. Joshua noted the insignia sewn to the man's shoulder.

"You're a major."

MacLean smiled. "Yes. And you're an embezzler. You and your professor friend didn't think you could just borrow three million dollars of university money without anyone noticing, did you, boy?"

Before Joshua could answer, the phone on the desk rang.

MacLean picked it up. "Hello?" He looked over. "It's for you." MacLean handed over the receiver.

"Hello?" said Joshua.

"I'm really sorry to do this," said Axel. "The man at my desk is Major Jack MacLean. He's army, but works with the CIA. I haven't told him anything about your traveling through time—"

"What do you want me to say?" Joshua couldn't believe Axel had put him in this situation. He was completely fucked. This man was probably well trained in interrogation. Of course the government had their hands all over a high energy collider laboratory. Probably half the staff were informants.

"I suggest you tell him the truth. It's up to him to believe it or not. Everything is under wraps for now, but if we don't cooperate they'll get the police and the securities regulator involved."

"There's nothing we can do about this?"

"No one has any record of your existence before one month ago. What did you expect?"

"Right. Okay, bye."

"Bye," said Axel.

Joshua handed the receiver to MacLean. "I have a few questions for you."

Joshua leaned back in his seat. "Ask away."

69

At the end of the corridor, Joshua had found a vending machine that dispensed coffee. It was a struggle to get it to accept his coins. Vending machines in the past, not just this one, were far, far more difficult to use. Still, coffee was cheap. Thirty—five cents for a decent sized cup.

He was even kind enough to get one for MacLean. It seemed that the man was little more than chasing his tail, half—convinced that Axel and Joshua were simply mad scientists. They'd spent the last hour going over everything. Joshua had tried to distract from the real story by over—explaining details, and invoking every bit of specialist vocabulary he knew.

But MacLean, despite Joshua's initial impression of him, was nobody's fool. He cut through the technical rigamarole and asked revealing questions. Even though Joshua's tale was ridiculous, he went along with it. For the time being, Joshua believed that MacLean accepted his story. They had bantered quite a bit about Los Alamos and Washington. Joshua hoped the coffee would assuage more of his worries. And where could Joshua hope to escape to? Better to co—operate with his potential captor.

As he approached Axel's office, Joshua stopped. MacLean was still on the phone. He held back, eavesdropping.

"And his story sounds completely batshit crazy—"

"I know," said Raven on the other end. "But he sounded convincing when he was drunk. And the phone, it shouldn't take long to figure—"

"Who cares? You forgot to take the part that plugs into the wall socket. Apparently Sinclair here destroyed it because we took his phone."

"Just great."

Joshua listened for a minute more, but the conversation was nothing but a recap of the interrogation. Then it changed to some other matter involving MacLean's travel expenses. Joshua decided he wouldn't get much more out of waiting. And the coffee was getting cold. So he walked in and sat down. Handed a cup to MacLean.

"Listen, I've got to go. I'll check in at eighteen hundred hours." He hung up the phone. "Well, Mr. Sinclair, you've stirred up quite a ruckus back in Langley with your talk of terrorist attacks and time travel."

"You don't seem convinced."

"There's a bunch of things I gotta get clear in my mind. Let's assume you're telling the truth. What if you visited your younger self and caused an accident?"

"Like what?"

"What if you killed your younger self? Isn't that a paradox?"

"I don't know. If it saves my father's life it was worth the risk. Like I've told you, I'm no expert at this. You're looking at things from the wrong perspective. I have no access to the collider data to explain what happened. But I know that I'm here. And I also know that once the battery on that phone runs out, all the knowledge on it will be inaccessible for the next twenty—five years. Unless you plan to spend an enormous amount of time and money attempting to reverse engineer it. I doubt those expenses would be approved by your superiors."

"I suppose your right." MacLean sipped his coffee. "The question is, what do we do with you? There's no point in locking you up. Making money isn't a crime."

Joshua glanced over at Axel's blackboard. He had to come clean. After taking a sip from the Styrofoam cup, he cleared his throat nervously. "Sure. Here's the whole story. I used to work for the CIA. Just for a few months back in 2002."

"Back...in 2002."

There was an awkward silence for a moment.

Joshua looked at him dead on. "Can I make a request?"

70

The hum of computers filled the waiting room.

Old computers. Huge mainframes that accepted data on spools of magnetic tape. Behind the waiting area were large machines, each the size of a dishwasher, stretching on for as far as the eye could see.

The room was big, easily the size of a football field. All filled with these sorts of machines. Some larger, some smaller. The front of the mainframe section was walled off by glass. A sergeant manned a desk by the main entrance. The waiting area was off to the side, a lot like a doctor's office. With chairs upholstered in some kind of red and off—colored orange pattern. And a table of old magazines.

Joshua figured places like this must exist in the future. But he doubted they accommodated such luxuries as dog—eared copies of the National Review. Axel was busy working away in a notepad filled with equations. While Joshua sat reading a

Time magazine with Oliver North on the cover. He reached the bottom of the first page before boredom set in.

Joshua closed the magazine on his lap. "Three days. This is crazy. I could do this on my laptop in fifteen minutes."

"Be grateful you got any time at all on these machines. They're jealously guarded. Usually there has to be a plane crash."

"You mean MacLean didn't tell you?"

"What?"

"I gave the facility a two million dollar donation for new equipment."

"Equipment?"

"They'll spend most of it on strippers, I'm sure. You don't think they're doing this out of the kindness of their heart? This is why they're not giving me a hard time. And the computer lab at Edwards Air Force base was more than happy to have us."

They'd flown in to California the day before. According to Axel, this was the most cutting—edge facility of its kind in the United States. It even had a partnership with IBM.

MacLean approached. Came over and shook hands. "We're ready to go. Follow me to the theatre. We have something to show you."

71

The projectionist sat at the back of the room.

Smoking.

The acrid smell invaded Joshua's nostrils. Several rows of plastic folding chairs had been set up. The room was illuminated by low lit lights.

"So," said MacLean, taking a seat, "we've input all the variables we know from the site. And from what you've told us. Based on your recollections. And the drawings you gave us. We've done several simulations. Estimating how much fuel remained in the jets and everything else. What you're about to see is a composite of all the possible simulations. The engineers who oversaw it say this is reliable to a 95% confidence interval."

He walked over and nodded to a man with horn—rimmed glasses. Sitting at a computer terminal with a monochrome monitor. And a panel with lots of blinking lights.

"Okay, roll it."

The lights went down.

Joshua glanced back. Saw the projectionist's cigarette smoke in the beam of light from the projector.

On the screen in front of them an old style green—on—black monochrome grid appeared. All Joshua could think about was that old movie Tron. With the motorcycles racing on a grid. Or Escape From New York. Speaking of which, the skyline of Manhattan appeared. Just as it was before 2001. The frame zoomed in to a green line drawing of the old World Trade Center.

Two green planes appeared. Flying towards the towers. And impacting.

The images repeated from several different angles. Showing the impact and damage in close up. A counter appeared in the corner of the screen, showing what happened second—by—second. The frame froze, moving in closer. Showed steel collapsing. And melting. The top part of the North Tower began to tilt to the right. Then debris began to fall, like cigarette ash.

"But then the buildings collapsed," said Joshua.

"We've factored in every variable we know," said MacLean, "but that outcome is impossible. There's no way that building could pancake."

The images changed. A different angle this time. Variables like wind, combustible materials, amount of jet fuel, and air pressure appeared in a list at the top of the screen.

On the South Tower, the top part of the building above the impact crater started to slope downwards.

The scene repeated, the variables changing each time. Each time the result was the same.

"So as you can see, if there was a structural failure, there is a ninety—five percent chance that the area above the impact site would start to lean forward."

Bits of debris fell out of the building from the bottom side of the tilting section.

MacLean walked up to the screen with a pointer. "The windows would have been blown out, and the floors would have sloped downwards due to the metal fatigue. These dots here represent elements ejected from the structure. The real danger would be for those people on the upper floors. With gravity, all the office equipment would fall out through the windows."

The lights came up. "That's it?" said Joshua. "That's the best you could come up with?"

"Our engineers have run the simulation hundreds of times in the last three days."

"But that isn't what happened. The buildings collapsed."

"I understand that. But the kind of steel they used...do you know that there's never ever been a skyscraper collapse in the history of mankind? Except under a controlled demolition. So I'll ask you—in the future, has any other building of this type collapsed?"

"No."

"So this only happened once? Sounds like magic to me. And of all the buildings built in those shit third world countries, the only one to collapse is right in the heart of New York City? Where all the cameras are aimed at it?"

"Yes, but—"

"And these terrorists happened to get so incredibly successful that they took out not just one, but both towers? Within half an hour of each other?"

"But that's—"

"It may not be impossible, but we're talking lottery ticket odds. Or worse."

"You're not getting me—"

"I don't care, son."

"But Afghanistan—"

"It's a very dangerous area. Controlled by the Soviets. With fighting between the commies and freedom fighters. I don't care how much money you have. There's no way we'd send you there. After getting to use our facility for a pet project for three days, you're lucky you're not being locked up."

"But—"

"We could talk to the SEC if you don't toe the line. You think you made all that money without some kind of insider knowledge?"

"What are you accusing us of?" said Axel. "Why don't...we just thank you for your time and efforts...right, Joshua?"

He refused to respond.

Axel looked down at his shoes. "Maybe it's time we left for the airport."

"Fine," said MacLean. "Just stay out of trouble."

72

One of Axel's dirty little secrets was that he cooked a really mean schnitzel. Tonight was Marianne's bridge night. With the other wives from the university physics department. Axel enjoyed the chance to cook. It gave him something to think about besides work. Also it gave them space in their relationship. And Marianne enjoyed taking the night off from the family. Making their marriage more bearable.

Axel's son Thomas had finished and gone upstairs to watch television. He and Joshua sat at the table, sipping coffee.

"That was excellent," said Joshua. "You have so many hidden skills."

"Well, we have to make do. American food isn't my favorite."

"But isn't it the same kind of food as in Germany?" Joshua thought about it for a moment. "I never once heard you complain about the food in Switzerland."

Axel shook his head. "Please...don't tell me about the future. It sounds like it's going to be nothing but problems."

"Well, I don't know. If it's your choice or not, I mean."

Axel put down his coffee mug. "I can't believe you asked MacLean to send you to Afghanistan. What were you thinking? Do you understand how dangerous that area is right now?"

Joshua sighed. "I have experience working with military operations. Years ago I was in the army."

"Sure, okay, but maybe in the future things are better over there—"

"Actually they're worse."

"Really? Worse than the threat of nuclear war?"

"That's a valid point. But we still have those weapons in the future. Can I tell you something?"

"Whatever you like."

"Promise you'll keep a secret?"

Axel looked over to his kitchen phone. Then he glanced to the radio. "I feel like some music. Is classical okay?"

Axel reached across the table and flicked on a transistor radio. Vivaldi came on. Axel raised the volume. Louder than expected. Then gestured to the ceiling. The room is probably bugged, at least that was what Joshua guessed his gestures meant. Axel stood up and moved to the center of the kitchen. Joshua followed.

"I can keep a secret, but I doubt our friend Major MacLean can."

"I'm going to Afghanistan."

"Excuse me?"

"We've got a bunch of money. I'll use it to infiltrate the Mujahideen group with al—Zawahiri."

Axel took a step back. "That sounds...insane."

"Why not? That's what Osama bin Laden did."

"Osama who?"

"Never mind. You don't need to know." Joshua rubbed his forehead. He thought for a moment about explaining how the son of a wealthy Saudi construction magnate had bought his way into a terrorist group with bags of money. But would it matter if he knew? "This is something I need to do for both of us."

"For both of us? Again you bring up...something. Just say it. Will you stop beating around the bush?"

"Right now there is a man living in Peshawar who has volunteered to help a group of Afghans resist their Soviet occupiers. Two years from now the Soviets will leave. However, America, which has been funding these fighters secretly through the CIA, will also withdraw."

"That seems sensible."

"Except that the power vacuum created by Soviet withdrawal will be filled by an autocratic Islamist government. The central powers in Afghanistan will allow a number of groups to conduct terrorist

293

trainings. They will be small in absolute numbers, but extraordinarily effective in spreading mayhem and destruction. One of these groups, opposed to an American military presence in Saudi Arabia after a brief war in Iraq in the year 1990, will hijack four airplanes. Both buildings in the World Trade Center complex will be destroyed. The Pentagon will also suffer damage. A fourth plane will crash in a field. In response to these attacks the NATO countries will invade Afghanistan and destroy the training camps. However, fearing the overthrow of the local government, the United States will withdraw its forces from Saudi, moving them to Bahrain. In an attempt to cover this up, a second invasion of Iraq will be arranged. This one costing far more lives and money than the one in 1990. Of course, no one in America, at the time, will know that. It will take another decade before people realize the government caved to terrorist demands."

Axel shook his head. "What you're telling me is hard to believe. It's so complicated. And these terrorists—if they're so well organized, what do you expect to do?"

"One man in their group is the key to all of this. He's their ideas man—an expert tactician named al—Zawahiri."

Axel sighed.

Joshua continued. "For years and years after these attacks, the government will search, desperately, for the people who've masterminded it.

They will even capture someone. A young man, at the time, no older than his mid—thirties. Who has been put up as a fall guy. However, the real person behind all this will go free. These details are not widely known, even in my time. The embarrassment of the way this matter was treated, and the trillions of dollars spent, have made it in everyone's interest to keep the truth from being...not exactly withheld.... It's been... de—emphasized."

"Trillions?"

"Yes."

"So they convicted the wrong man?"

"But that's the problem. They haven't convicted him. Instead, they've kept him under arrest without a trial. Possibly because they fear the prosecution might be unable to make the case. Most of the actual hijackers died in the attack."

"It sounds like a big mess."

"That it is."

Axel thought about it for a moment. The winter part of The Four Seasons came on. "I think I've seen this movie before. Except those people were going back in time to kill Hitler."

"What do you expect me to do?"

"For starters, you'll probably be killed. You have just over a week before you'll be returned—"

"Assuming this procedure works. Which we do not know if it will. I could be stuck here for the rest of my life."

"Correct. If it works. But that's a far safer bet than Soviet—occupied Afghanistan. You'll probably have a long career ahead of you in science. Or finance. Or you might have a family."

Joshua paced back and forth before stopping and giving Axel a long, hard look. "Do you have any idea the amount of ionizing radiation my body has been exposed to in that collider accident? Or what dosage I'll get on the way back? What makes you so confident about my future? For all I know, I might be dead in two years from thyroid cancer."

"I'm an optimist."

A thumping came from the ceiling.

"Daddy! Mommy said you have to put me to bed now."

"Coming." Axel turned to go upstairs. He probably had the only child in the world who wanted to go to sleep early on a regular basis. "I've got to put my son to bed."

Joshua grabbed his wrist. Axel stopped mid—stride. "In September, 2001, my father will be killed at the Pentagon. Your son will die at the World Trade Center in New York."

Axel ripped away Joshua's hand like it was diseased. "You feel good about telling me this?" He rushed out.

73

Thomas had already pulled the GoBot polyester sheets over him by the time Axel walked in the room and sat down on the bed. "Ready to go to sleep?" he said.

"Are you going away, daddy?"

"Where did you hear that?"

"I heard mommy talking to her friend on the phone. She said the government has a job for you. You aren't going to leave us are you, daddy?"

Axel looked at his son. "No. Never."

As he did every night, Axel switched into German and told his son a bedtime story. Even though Thomas couldn't speak the native language of his father, he could at least understand it. Axel believed daily exposure was important.

But as he told the story, he held back tears. Knowing the future. He could put a hold on all the accounts. Cut Joshua off from funding. Maybe even lock him in the basement. It might even be possible to get him committed to a mental institution. It was after all, for his own safety.

Or he could turn a blind eye.

When the story was finished, Axel flicked off the lights, returned to the kitchen and sat down. He looked at Joshua.

"Fine," said Axel, "what do you want to do?"

74

The entire street was low—rent. Vinyl—siding clad houses, most in various states of disrepair. It wasn't all that far from the Royal Castle Motel. Where Joshua had spent his formative nights in 1987. This was one of the few neighborhoods on the south side filled with Eastern European immigrants.

Lots of the people here were from the Balkans. Or what, in this time period, was known as Yugoslavia. Lots of Croatians and Serbs. People plotting the overthrow of Tito's regime. For all their ambitions, Joshua knew the communist—lite government's secret police had infiltrated most of the diaspora groups. The best thing they could do was wait it out. Joshua wondered if his situation wasn't analogous.

He shrugged these feelings off as he approached the green siding—clad house. The place was dingy, with what looked like bullet holes near a front window, and abandoned children's toys scattered throughout the front yard. He stepped over a tricycle and turned onto a narrow walkway between the green house and its neighbors.

Joshua stopped at a side storm door. Opened it and knocked at a white wooden door with peeling paint. He didn't like the alley. It made him vulnerable to attack from three sides. His military tactician mind had returned with a vengeance. Something that had lay dormant for the past fifteen years. The scientist in him was being submerged. He'd started doing pushups and working out. Every single day. To get his body back in shape.

After a minute of waiting, the door opened. Joshua was greeted by an unkempt eastern European man in his mid—sixties. From the smell of his breath, it seemed vodka was his main source of caloric intake.

The man examined Joshua for a moment, silently. "You are Sinclair?"

"Yes. And you are Sergei?"

The man nodded. "Come."

"Thank you for taking on this assignment," said Joshua as he followed Sergei down a rickety set of wooden stairs.

"No problem. But it wasn't easy to get what you asked. I'm afraid I'll need an extra thousand."

"Fine."

Joshua had been told to expect this. Sergei didn't like doing jobs for Americans. He had no compunction about shaking them down for as much as possible. It had taken quite the snooping around just to make contact with him. He was well known in his field. Fortunately Joshua was resourceful. Tracking down the underground economy was difficult in the days before the internet.

At least he wouldn't be found out easily.

The basement was unfinished. Along one wall stood some printing equipment. Opposite was a cluttered desk with decaying wooden chairs on either side. Next to a rusting oil—fired furnace. Across the room, next to a workbench, was a line of printing equipment.

Sergei beckoned Joshua to sit down at the desk. Made his best attempt to appear welcoming.

Joshua produced an envelope, passing it to Sergei who took it without counting the money. There was little worry the amount of cash was incorrect. Then Joshua took out a wallet and tossed down some more bills with Benjamin Franklin on them.

Sergei opened a drawer. Put in the money and took out a passport. "Fortunately you've got the right accent."

He passed Joshua the navy blue booklet. It said "CANADA" on the front.

Joshua flicked through it. Inside was his picture, with all new details.

Sergei raised his eyebrows. "It is satisfactory?"

75

Despite his CIA training, Joshua hadn't spotted the van. And why would he? It was an old Ford Econoline. Even in this era, it had to be at least fifteen years old.

Large and blue, the side of it was covered by a composite airbrushed portrait of Mark Hammill, Carrie Fisher, and an X—wing fighter jet. In the corner near a rear window, Obi—wan Kenobi fought a light—saber duel with Darth Vader.

It wasn't the kind of van you'd expect government contractors to do surveillance from. Which was why Raven had chosen it.

Inside, she looked over at Denny, the photographer. He got a good shot of Joshua saying goodbye to Sergei. And kept snapping away as Joshua walked off.

"Do you want us to pursue?" asked Roger, the sound guy. "I didn't get anything above ground. Too much interference."

"And in the basement?"

"Unbelievable," said the audio guy. "We've got everything. Perfectly clean."

"Looks like we'll be able to knock off early," said the photographer.

Raven shook her head. "I don't know, maybe we should follow him. But I'll need to find another vehicle. This one...is a bit too obvious for a tailing."

"You got any plans?" said Denny to Roger.

"Well, actually—"

"I've got this extra ticket to the Frank Sinatra Junior concert tonight."

"I'll be fine." Roger turned to Raven. "I've got some chatter from the passport forger. You speak Russian, don't you?"

In the basement Sergei was already on the telephone.

"Yes," he said to his Russian colleague. "I've made the hand off.... No, I'm sure there will be no problems tracking him...."

He hung up and smiled. Went back to counting his money.

76

The greyhound trip from Chicago to Detroit had been long and tiring. But it offered the easiest way of traveling without being noticed by MacLean or anyone else. Joshua crossed the border on a local city bus through a tunnel under the St. Claire river. The customs official didn't bother to ask about his passport. The driver's license was good enough. They probably thought he was heading over to the strip clubs. He spent the night in a cheap Windsor hotel. The next morning he got the first train out.

It was a long, ten—hour train journey, with a layover in Toronto. The weather was cold when he arrived in Montreal. If a CIA agent had bothered to follow him, it certainly would be arduous. Joshua had plenty of time to examine his fellow passengers. And had followed every technique he knew to avoid being shadowed.

For two whole days he wandered around Montreal, playing tourist. Trying to get his bearings. And researching the ex—patriot Afghan community in the city. He had been told it was the largest in North America. Joshua believed it offered the best chance of finding people who were sympathetic to what he wanted to do.

On the third day the snow started. He took a bus to the north end of the city. Along with a dozen or so other passengers Joshua got off at a lonely corner of an intersection bordered by parking lots. Tall modernist apartment blocs in the distance. Some of the disembarking passengers carried on conversations in French. Others in different languages. The only commonality was that none of them were white people. Joshua certainly stood out.

He separated from the other passengers and headed to the nearby strip mall. Crossing an empty parking lot in the newly fallen snow. The area could best be described as affordable. Not quite yet dilapidated. An area for new immigrants and ethnic restaurants. Far from the metro. And the glitzy nightclubs of downtown. The kind of area that allowed for cheap living.

Ahead of him was a small group from the bus. Three or four people, all dressed in Afghan—style clothing. They walked towards one of the storefronts. The group entered a nondescript establishment—what might be a convenience store or an H & R Block. Except that the sign, below the french lettering, was in Pashto. Despite his experience in the Middle East, he couldn't read it.

Joshua surveyed the sign. It was a mosque. Joshua backed off. He knew going inside would generate too many questions. Especially since it was time for afternoon prayers. He walked away.

A few stores down he found another sign in Pashto and French—

"Cuisine Afghan."

A bell attached to the door jingled as Joshua entered. The place was devoid of customers. It looked like it might have been a Kentucky Fried Chicken in a former life. The booths were suspiciously white with red upholstery.

Joshua approached a man and a woman behind the counter.

"Excuse me, do you speak English?"

77

McGill University was, like the city of Montreal, a strange beast. A mixture of classical and avant—garde. Too often, though, avant—garde meant 'ugly modernist building put up in the 1970s.'

As the sun set, Joshua was headed to one of those buildings. He turned off Sherbrooke Street, walking through the main gate, as the final rays of sunlight stretched across the lawn that was dotted with squirrels. Foraging between patches of melting snow. He looked at the leaflet that had brought him here.

An event by an Afghan lawyer named Waladi. Who was giving a speech about the need to get the Soviets out of Afghanistan. Part of the anti—occupation efforts. He was well—connected to the Afghani royal family. Many of their members had come to Canada. Joshua held the suspicion that it was the best way for him to pass into Afghanistan undiscovered. These people needed his money. He figured, in exchange for it, they'd be willing to look the other way. Perhaps grant him superior access, in a way the American government couldn't.

Maybe.

But Joshua knew he would suffer from the fact that he didn't speak any of the Afghan languages.

He passed by some students exiting a stunning Victorian—era building. Heading left, he approached a monument to seventies architectural excess. The complex looked like it had been ripped out of a 70s science fiction movie.

This was the Leacock Building. Named after a Canadian author who wrote humorous short stories about small town folk. As far from science fiction as you could get.

He found a bulletin board in the foyer. Listing the meetings and speeches for that night. He headed to the main auditorium.

Passing through a set of double doors, Joshua found himself in a room that could hold at least four hundred. Today, though, there were only about thirty people scattered about.

At the podium stood a middle aged Afghan man, Waladi, presumably. Giving a speech in lightly accented English. Dressed in a suit. Like you'd expect from a lawyer. Joshua walked down and took a seat in the front.

"Which brings me," said Waladi, "to the issue of rebuilding our society. It is not enough to plan for victory in battle. We must also plan for stability after our occupiers have left."

As the lawyer droned on, Joshua fought off exhaustion. He'd been going for three days straight. This man was his best—and only—hope. After the lecture was over, Joshua stayed in his seat. Watching a small group of Afghan students crowd around Waladi, asking questions.

Just as the lawyer was about to make an escape, Joshua walked to the exit, cornering the man. "Excuse me, I just wanted to thank you for your speech tonight."

Waladi smiled modestly. "Oh, thank you." He was overly eager to get out of the room. Almost twitchy. Joshua realized that the guy probably had to go to the bathroom.

"I was wondering if there's any way I could make a donation."

"Well, at any branch of the Royal Bank or the Bank of Montreal. If you could wait a minute, I'll get you the information—"

"Actually, I was thinking about an amount a bit larger than that."

78

The Pashtun restaurant was nice.

Occupying a street corner at the northern edge of the Plateau neighborhood. Joshua was impressed by the decor. It looked...pricey. And well put together. A far cry from the places he'd seen in Montreal North. The dining room filled with the scents and smells of Afghan cooking, and tea.

They'd finished an excellent meal of lamb kebab and bolani. Followed by mantu. After that, they sipped tea.

It was the next day following Waladi's lecture. Joshua sat across the table from him and a young man named Fazil Tahirzai, dressed in prep school style clothing. The guy wouldn't be out of place in a group of graduate students. In fact, Joshua wondered if he wasn't going to school at McGill. The guy spoke perfectly fluent English. Without an accent. Obviously the product of various international schools.

Most of the time during the meal was spent discussing the young man's back story. Working as a scientist. Joshua, too, had explained who he was. Except that he'd adjusted most of his life story to fit the times. It wasn't a lie, but it wasn't completely the truth, either.

After the last dishes were taken away, and they were all sipping tea, Joshua leaned forward. "Mr. Tahirzai, I understand the troubles your family has endured—"

Tahirzai grinned. "I doubt you'd fully understand."

"Very well, but I want you to know that I'm not doing this to reinstate your family as the reining Afghan monarchy. I'm doing this for the future of your country."

Waladi and Tahirzai glanced at each other nervously. As if to say, is this guy for real?

"That said," continued Joshua, "I appreciate you giving me your time."

"Time is something I have plenty of these days."

Waladi cut in. "If I could speak frankly, what kind of donation did you have in mind?" Waladi knew that, despite being a prince, Tahirzai wasn't a good negotiator.

"One hundred million dollars."

Tahirzai and Waladi's eyes widened. They looked over at each other with almost comic incredulity.

"Thirty million to be pledged to reconstruction after the Soviets leave. The remainder will be at your discretion."

"Our discretion?" said Waladi.

Joshua took a sip of tea. "I'm assuming that you'll use it for military purposes. However, it has the advantage of not being filtered through the Pakistani secret service."

That should get their interest, thought Joshua. He knew all too well the influence of Pakistan on its western neighbor's politics. Despite what was drawn on the maps, there was basically no border between the two countries. If you looked at the population of Pakistan, almost all of it was clustered in a very narrow band of cities. Close to the border with India. The vast tribal area to the west was officially considered part of Pakistan. But unofficially, it more—or—less belonged to the many Pashtun tribes that moved between the two countries with ease. Fortunately, the Soviets had yet to bomb over the border. Content to simply occupy the Afghanistan side. But it was, as they say, uncontrollable.

Tahirzai looked over at Joshua, contemplating the bombshell that had just been dropped. "And you have no problems giving this away? No questions asked?"

"I have a couple of conditions," said Joshua. "They should be easy to fulfill."

"Really?" said the young man.

"First, am I right that the fight for your country has resulted in a flood of volunteers from other Islamic states?"

Waladi nodded. "This is true. More than twenty thousand, at last estimate."

"One of them," said Joshua, "has caught my attention. I'd like to talk with him."

"That sounds possible," said Waladi. "A meeting could be arranged with those working for our freedom. Perhaps in Karachi or Islamabad. If we can get them away from the front lines."

Joshua nodded. And leaned forward, lowering his voice. "Which brings me to my second request. I want to see what the insurgents are doing up close. I want to take a trip into Afghanistan."

Tahirzai and Waladi burst out laughing. Simultaneously.

Joshua was taken aback. "What's so funny?"

Waladi smiled. "Who do you think we are? The CIA? Some kind of battlefield tourist company?"

Tahirzai also shook his head. "We're advocates for the Afghani people. We solicit donations. Raise awareness. Petition politicians." He took a sip of tea, almost to control his laughter. "We don't coordinate strikes on Soviet air bases."

"And," said Waladi, "even if we did bring you into the country, how exactly would you blend in with blond hair and blue eyes?"

Joshua thought for a moment. "I shouldn't be telling you this, but I have experience working in Afghanistan."

"How?" said Tahirzai

"I used to work for the CIA." There. It was on the table. He was ready to be exposed.

Tahirzai sat up in his chair. "Really?"

316

"Only for a year. But I know that desert and a lot of those caves. And I can handle myself in combat. I have experience as a sniper. And in para—trooping. And limited experience dealing with the local tribesmen. Through a translator, of course."

"Why don't you ask your friends in the CIA for a plane ticket?"

"It's complicated."

Tahirzai slumped back in his chair.

"It always is."

Joshua reached down under the table and pulled up a briefcase. It was heavy. He struggled to lay it on the table. Moving everything in front of him aside, he grabbed a key, attached to a band around his wrist. Unlocked it.

Inside was only one thing—bundles of thousand dollar bills. The case was completely full.

Tahirzai eyed the money like a hungry lion.

"Now," said Joshua, "will this make up for a few complications?"

79

Pan—American Flight 52 from Heathrow was a brief jaunt. But Joshua hadn't slept on the Montreal—London leg. Filled with nervous energy as he was.

It was two days after the restaurant meeting.

The three of them, Waladi, Tahirzai, and Joshua, had taken the overnight to Europe. Joshua had booked the flight immediately upon returning to his hotel.

Waladi had been surprised, and initially had refused. But Joshua held firm, dangling the money like a carrot. He'd even handed some cash over to Waladi for safe—keeping—but not for deposit.

There was almost ten million dollars in that suitcase.

The day before the flight, Joshua wanted to book accommodations, but Waladi insisted that he do it himself, through his lawyer. So instead Joshua waited. Thought through his plan.

They'd agreed to go to Berlin, first. Meet with an ex—pat British lawyer who Waladi worked with in Europe. They had reached London that morning and transferred. Around 11:30 they took off for Germany. Another hour added to the journey. Not much.

The first class section was mostly empty, being a Tuesday morning. Waladi and Tahirzai took the window seats, while Joshua stretched out across the aisle. He was making up for the sleepless night.

When he began snoring, Tahirzai looked over. He nudged Joshua. No response. Back in his seat, Tahirzai turned back to Waladi. "I think he's asleep," he said in Pashto.

Waladi rolled his eyes. "What are you worried about? You think he speaks our language?"

"No. But after the last few days nothing would surprise me. Best to be careful."

"I spoke to Steinberg before we boarded. He'll be ready to meet in his Berlin office first thing."

"Yes, best if our friend here is a bit jet lagged. There's a better chance of him speaking the truth."

"You think he's hiding something?"

"How could he not be? What if it's some sort of Soviet trap? Some way of embarrassing us in front of the Americans?"

Waladi shifted in his seat. He found Tahirzai bright, but inexperienced. Sometimes he compensated with paranoia. Not surprising, given what his family had gone through. There were times when he'd seen Tahirzai's temper erupt. Anger rising out of the fact that he had no control over his country. Or more correctly, his family's former country.

Waladi yawned. "What if.... What if.... What if.... This man is a crazy American. He's been deluded by too many John Wayne movies. This is his way of being a cowboy. He knows his way around Afghanistan. Now he wants to set something right. I have no problem with that."

"But if he betrays us—"

"So what if he's a Soviet agent? As long as we get his money first."

The landing announcement came on.

Waladi leaned back. "Que sera sera."

80

The landing at Templehof was rough. No doubt due to the rain clouds overhead. They had lingered after thunderstorms a few hours earlier. But, according to the flight attendant, it was relatively warm for a late November day. Almost fifteen degrees Celsius as the Boeing 707 taxied to the terminal.

The tires screeched as they touched down. The ancient aircraft's pressurization was wrecking havoc on Joshua's hearing ability. Not to mention the seat upholstery, which had survived the 1970s.

No wonder Pan—American had eventually gone under.

They made their way through customs with relative ease. Since they'd all packed lightly, the three of them managed to squeeze into a single taxi cab.

Joshua looked out the window as the neighborhoods of West Berlin passed by. They took the long route to the center of town. Right past the

Berlin wall. Joshua wondered if the cab driver was trying to show off. Such a strange city, he thought, catching a glimpse of Checkpoint Charlie.

The Cold War world. Divided by silly ideologies.

Then again, if it happened to smart, educated people back in this time, it could just as easily happen in the future, couldn't it?

An hour and a half after they landed, their taxi pulled up to the steps of an ornate pre—war building. They got out, and the cab driver was about to retrieve their luggage when Waladi told the man to wait. They wouldn't be long.

He turned to Joshua. "Mr. Steinberg would like to talk to you briefly before we head on to the hotel."

"If you insist."

"We do."

They headed up to the third floor where a stout German secretary ushered them in to a luxuriously appointed office.

Completely sealed from the racket of typewriters coming from the outer lobby. The walls were lined with legal texts. They sunk down into plush leather seats. Set off in a corner of the office, far from the lawyer's desk. With windows that looked out over a park across the street.

They waited as the secretary brought in a tea set, pouring them each a cup. After a delay of a couple of minutes, from a side door there appeared David Steinberg, barrister and solicitor. A balding man in his late forties, he looked elegant in a tailored suit. Probably from Savile Row, thought Joshua. Accented with expensive cuff links.

"Gentlemen, thank you all for making this journey. My apologies for keeping you waiting." Steinberg took an empty seat next to Tahirzai.

It dawned on Joshua that the man was probably a Jew. An interesting choice of representation for a Muslim group.

Waladi smiled. "It's good to see you again, too."

"So this is your charge...Mr. Sinclair. The pleasure is all mine." Steinberg reached over and shook hands.

"Nice to meet you," said Joshua. "I assume you want to know all about me."

Steinberg poured himself a cup of tea. "No. Not at all. You're a man who turned up out of thin air with a promise of a hundred million dollars. No social insurance number. Credit card history. Where did you get your passport, by the way? I'm assuming you're not Canadian."

Joshua put down his tea. "You find my situation unusual?"

"I've seen weirder."

Tahirzai leaned forward. "He just wants to ask you some questions. Before you meet the higher ups in the organization."

"So," said Joshua, "you're the public face of the Mujahideen?"

"One of them."

An awkward silence descended over the conversation.

"Tell me," said Steinberg, "is this your first time in Berlin?"

"No," said Joshua, "I used to work for the CIA and the army."

"Yes, I've heard. You certainly picked the right place to attract an awful lot of attention." Steinberg got up and moved over to a nearby cabinet. "Someone suggested you might be a Soviet agent."

From the cabinet Steinberg removed a small gauge pistol.

"But I don't believe the Russians would ever be that sloppy. They would never hand over six million dollars in a briefcase. In a restaurant on the Plateau de Montreal." Steinberg took the gun and handed it to Joshua. "No, I think there's something careless about you. Careless...but genuine."

Joshua looked at the pistol. "What's this?"

Steinberg beckoned him to take the weapon. "I always arrange insurance for my clients."

81

Joshua kept silent for most of the trip.

He knew the more he talked, the greater the chance he'd say something absurd.

Of the four of them in the taxi—Steinberg had joined them—Waladi and Tahirzai had elected to stay at the Hilton.

Joshua moved to join them when Steinberg pulled him back. "We've selected a different hotel for you. If that's okay?"

"Sure." This was awkward. Joshua watched as the other men unloaded their luggage. "So," said Joshua, after they had departed, "where am I going?"

"We wanted to make sure you had adequate privacy."

"No shit. They're that afraid of who I might represent?"

"It might be in all our best interests if you had some time on your own. To think about what you're doing.

Away from our influence. And also my associates would like to be free to socialize with others."

"Away from my prying eyes?"

"Possibly."

Joshua looked out the window as they passed by Potsdamer Platz. "To think how half this city is under totalitarian rule."

"We are cursed to live in interesting times."

"Tell me," said Joshua, "why would a group of radical Muslims hire a Jew to represent them?"

"I wouldn't call them all that radical. They're freedom fighters."

"For now."

"Let's just say, I give their arguments a degree of credibility they might not have if a Mujahideen fighter showed up at a press conference."

Joshua grinned. "You've got this all figured out."

"To some degree."

The taxi pulled up to a building with a 1930s Bauhaus exterior. It was absolutely stunning. A grid of white on black. Completely distinct from all the buildings around it. Joshua was surprised to see such architectural experimentation had survived the war. The door swung open and Joshua got out. The driver already had his bags waiting.

Before the cab left, Steinberg leaned out the window. "One more thing, Mr. Sinclair."

"Yes?"

"Be careful. West Berlin isn't as safe as it seems on the surface."

"West Berlin." Joshua still hadn't gotten used to the city name. "Unbelievable."

"I don't want to alarm you, but I know people," Steinberg looked around suspiciously, "who know people. Who like to keep an eye on things for the opposition. And I've heard they've got their eye on you."

"Who? Where?"

"Those are questions only you can answer. In the meantime, relax. See the sights. Go to the zoo."

Joshua started to leave. "Or the wall."

"One more thing, Sinclair—"

"Yeah?"

"Don't shoot anyone unless you've got an escape route."

82

The Hotel Ellington was beautiful. With elaborate decorative metal grills in the lobby. However, despite this, it felt due for renovations. Joshua took a dingy old elevator up to the seventh floor. There was no bellhop available. So Joshua carried his suitcase on his own.

It might be better to ditch it for something more practical. He'd only bought it to make an impression on Tahirzai. That he wasn't just some kind of homeless person.

The clerk had promised a view away from the street. Much quieter. Which would allow him to get at least some sleep.

Exiting the elevator, he found his room at the very end of the hallway. He unlocked the door with an old—style metal room key. The door swung open, cutting through the darkness. Joshua switched on the lights, catching a glimpse of movement towards the bed.

The curtains were drawn. The housekeeping staff wouldn't normally do that, would they? Joshua's hair stood on end. Why leave the room in such a gloomy state?

He felt for the pistol Steinberg had given him.

Taking it out, he examined it. A Walther PPQ. No safety. The kind of gun a policeman might carry. He didn't even know if it had bullets in it.

He moved forward cautiously—aiming the weapon toward the bed—until his saw who was in it.

"What are you doing here?"

A naked Raven had wrapped herself in the blankets. She scowled when she saw the gun. "Put that away. Mister."

"Is this your idea of 'covert operations'?"

She smiled. "I thought I'd try the 'good cop' approach."

Joshua put the pistol back in the holster. Released the clip and emptied the chamber. Put it on the bedside table. Then sat down on the bed. "I thought you slept with me last time just for information."

Raven tried to kick him away, unsuccessfully. "I'm not that kind of girl. If I wanted information out of you, I've got a pharmacy of medications in my purse." She sat up. The sheets fell away as she got close to him.

He looked down at her naked body.

She nuzzled him with her feet under the

332

blanket. "I slept with you because I'm single and I thought you were cute."

"The fact we met in a bar had nothing to do with it?"

"Nothing."

Joshua pushed her down and kissed her deeply.

83

Joshua suckled on Raven's erect nipples. They were larger than he'd seen in a while.

They'd been making love for an hour or so now, much better without the corrupting influence of alcohol.

And it was incredibly hot.

He had thought about her quite a bit since they last saw each other. And yet...it was all so whirlwind. He worried he was falling in love with her. The woman from the past.

"You are not," she said.

"I doubt it."

"Tell me, what would you like to do?"

"I don't know."

"You're American, aren't you? You could just come back to the States."

"That's not possible."

"Why not?"

"Because...after this is over I have to go... underground."

"Where? And what is so important about you taking all your money and heading off to Afghanistan?"

"You know?"

"About your plans? Yes. Quite a bit. It sounds crazy. Whatever it is you're trying to do. You're going to get killed."

"No, but I am going to disappear. For quite some time."

"And do what?"

"Go back to my old life. As a scientist."

"Your not still talking that line of bullshit are you?"

"It's my job. This escapade in Afghanistan...it's just what I do to make the world a better place."

"Uh—huh." Raven stood up and opened the curtains. Watched the sun set over West Berlin.

"You've been here before?" he asked.

"Many times," she said, lighting a cigarette. "Often for work. I spent quite a bit of time recently in Germany."

Joshua grabbed himself a drink from the mini—bar. "So, why'd you show up here? Just aching to get to Berlin?"

"Somebody thought it would be a good idea to keep an eye on you."

"'Somebody' meaning MacLean."

A grin spread across Raven's face.

336

"And you know the territory better than anyone else, right?"

Raven kissed him on the cheek. "We have lots of agents in the city. I come here to coordinate things. When they need extra help."

"Are you planning to stop me?"

Raven exhaled a plume of smoke. "I don't plan on doing anything. Think of me as a disinterested observer."

Joshua emptied a miniature bottle of vodka into a glass, and added some ginger ale. "Because I can stick my neck out without approval of Congress."

"For the record, I never said that."

"But you people like to see me giving money to these guys. Since, for the time being, they're on our side."

"The government can't do everything. Haven't you heard of Reaganomics?"

He opened up the desk drawer and pulled out a map of the city. "This is my first time in Berlin."

"Really? It's not that complicated. As long as you stay on the west side of the wall."

Joshua got back on the bed and snuggled up to her. "Want to go to the zoo?"

84

The next morning Joshua and Raven had breakfast in their room. Rye bread with lox and poached eggs. The coffee was good. Joshua was having a rough morning after downing a few too many mini bottles the night before. He didn't mind drinking. Who knows how long he'd have to wait for Steinberg and Tahirzai. They'd put him in a holding pattern.

So what if Raven wanted to be his girlfriend for the day? He was happy with that. After taking a shower they looked at the map. Walk through the Tiergarten. Then end up at the zoo.

Joshua and Raven exited the hotel holding hands. Happy. "You know," he said, "you're kind of fun to be with."

"So you admit it."

"And you're not married?"

She looked at the ground. "I used to be."

"I see."

"So you have a family?"

"Yes. You could say that."

They walked out the front.

"Should we take a cab?" he asked.

"In Berlin? I always do. I've never figured out the U—bahn. Or the S—bahn. Or whatever they call the subway over here."

Joshua walked to the curb and attempted to wave down a taxi.

In the distance he saw a Mercedes cab switch on its indicator lamp. But before it could reach them a blue Lada, parked no more than ten feet away, swerved in front of them, cutting off the taxi's path. Both side doors opened.

Out of the front seat—

—a burly Russian thug leapt out. Another man, older, leaned towards them from the backseat. Joshua saw an Uzi machine gun in his hand.

"What's going on here?" said Raven. It was only then that she saw the man holding the Uzi.

Mendel. "Won't you join me again, Ms. Qaddumi?"

"Get in," said the thug pushing them into the back, "or we will not hesitate to kill you right here. In broad daylight."

85

Joshua filled with panic.

This was not how he wanted to die. In an East Berlin office building where they tortured people. But he could do nothing as the door was shut and locked behind him. Locked from the outside, like a police car.

Joshua looked over, past Raven to Mendel. His face had the cold clear lines of the Russian peasantry. Someone who had seen plenty of killing. And had few compunctions about having to do it himself.

When Joshua looked over again, Mendel had replaced the Uzi with a pistol. Aimed so that he could shoot either of them at waist level. A very nasty angle. The kind of angle that requires a knowledgeable surgeon. An angle from which, even if stopped, no one outside the vehicle would notice he was carrying a weapon.

By the look on Raven's face, it seemed she, too, had realized the situation was hopeless.

As the guard in the front seat shut his door, the car sped off. Mendel was completely focused on Raven who he spoke to in German. "We're just taking you two over for a little talk—"

"Like hell you are," replied Raven in perfect German. "You'll have half of Washington bearing down on you, pig!"

"I'm going to be nice and put my gun away. For the sake of international relations."

The car sped through a mostly deserted Potsdamer Platz. Turning a corner, the car passed the Berlin Wall—covered in graffiti and brightly covered artwork.

Mendel laid his gun down by his side near the door. Something about Raven calling him a pig made him relax.

Raven dug through her purse. This got the attention of Mendel. He tightened his grip on the gun. But all she pulled out was lipstick and a compact.

"I might as well look good for your interrogators," she said.

He relaxed, turning back to the window.

She examined her lips for a moment. With Mendel distracted—

—she turned a small knob on the front of the compact.

Joshua watched her out of the corner of his eye.

The mirror darkened. It changed to some kind of translucent screen. A grid appeared. Faded yellow. An overlay, like a cell phone camera. Only much weaker. The light was reflected from a small hole at the front of the compact. Like an old fashioned reflex camera.

She adjusted the knobs. Two neon green sights appeared. One vertical, the other horizontal. Crossing dead center in the grid. She aimed the cross—hairs right at the driver's neck—

Raven clicked a button and the grid completely disappeared. She waited as they sped down the road. Holding the compact steady. Waiting until the Lada took a corner just a little faster than it should. A hard left turn.

Raven pointed her lipstick tube at the driver and twisted.

Firing a bullet, from her hand. From where the lipstick nub had been. Joshua saw the driver's neck explode in a mess of red. Not all of it blood.

"Get down," screamed Raven.

Joshua ducked into a crash position, covering his head.

The car swerved onto the sidewalk. Hit the curb. Took flight. Careened wildly into one of the shops.

Slamming into the front of a butcher. Beef carcasses and sausages flew everywhere. Joshua held on as he banged off the passenger seat. Was this the end?

The front of the Lada collided with the metal and glass counter.

Behind which two butchers, in full apron, jumped out of the way. In a panic they raced to the back, scrambling out the back door. The car dragged the counter across the store, smashing against a wall of sauerkraut jars.

The last thing Joshua remembered before passing out.

86

Joshua never went completely unconscious, but for a moment he felt completely stunned.

Disorientated.

He wanted to move, but his body felt heavy, like it was swimming against a rip current. All he could do was lean back, try and let the dizziness stop.

Raven came around first. She leaned forward, pulling herself up. Despite the impact, she quickly got her bearings. Pushed herself forward. Looked in the front.

The driver and the guard were unconscious.

She saw Mendel's gun at her feet. She reached down to grab it—

—as he grabbed her wrist. The two of them grappled. She struggled, trying to rip his arms away.

"Stop it, you fool," he said in German.

Raven maneuvered herself around. Twisting her legs up, she kicked the end of her stiletto heel into the side of Mendel's head.

It only took one kick.

His skull connected with the metal of the door frame. Which had bent out of shape. He flopped forward and vomited all over his lap. When he was done heaving, he fell to his side, eyes closed. Raven poked at his body. He was out. She pulled the pistol away from him.

Behind her Joshua coughed.

"Can you move?" she said.

He hacked some more. Then moved forward. "I think so."

"You aren't coughing blood, are you?"

Joshua looked down at his hand covered in saliva. "I'm okay."

She tried Mendel's door, but there was no way the metal frame, bent out of shape as it was, would budge. And they'd have to climb through his vomit.

Joshua tried his window. It rolled down easily. "The only part of this Lada that works," he said. Climbing out the window he discovered the car was surrounded by a pile of beef carcasses. Dislodged when they crashed. He couldn't get over the damage to the store. The Lada had completely wrecked the deli counter. They'd nearly died. No one else seemed to be around, or under, the mangled vehicle. It was a lucky shot.

The driver and the guard in the front had taken most of the impact.

"Come on," said Raven, grabbing Joshua's arm. People were already crowding around the sidewalk in front of the crash site. In the far distance came police sirens. Getting closer. "We've got to go."

Joshua looked down at her feet. Raven was wearing high heels. "You're going to be okay in those?"

"I'll be fine. Let's go."

Over the protests of a man in the crowd, they left the scene. Turned down an alleyway. Raven knew the city far better than Joshua. He was lost by the time they took the second corner. After a couple more minutes, they found a pay phone.

Grabbing the receiver, Raven put in a coin and dialed a number. "Hello? Gunter? It's me. I need to make a booking."

87

Mendel came around. He wiped the vomit off his face and sat up. He had no memory of throwing up. What had happened? They'd crashed. He looked at his watch. Twenty minutes had passed.

Turning around he saw the crowd on the sidewalk. Not good. He had to get out of here. Gazing at the onlookers, he didn't see any police. Good.

Ugh, the stink of it all.

Leaning forward, he surveyed the scene. Two butchers were cowering in the corner of the shop, by the door. One of them had a telephone receiver in hand. The other saw him stir. Started to move towards the car.

Mendel leaned in front. Checked pulses.

Both his colleagues were dead. He looked over the blood drying on their bodies. There was nothing he could do for them now. His face remained expressionless. He had to keep his emotions in check. There would be time to deal with his feelings later.

Right now, he had to escape. He felt his ankle brush up against something. Looking to the floor, he saw the gleam of metal....

He reached down.

And picked up his Uzi.

Ms. Qaddumi. She'd tried to grab his pistol. But the machine gun—in her panic she forgot it! This was an especially fortunate event.

Mendel leaned forward into the front seat. Between his colleagues he found the radio phone. He picked up the receiver. There was still a tone. There were plenty of people in the city who could help him

"Control, this is Berlin LC five—nine—five...."

88

Joshua paced nervously by the pay phone. He wanted to go...anywhere...some cafe. As long as they were out of sight. Turning around he looked at Raven, who was still nodding to the speaker on the other end. Silence as she took instructions. He started pacing again. How could they stay out in the open for so long.

For all his time in the army and the stint in the CIA, he'd never operated in an urban theater. What if their were spotters? Snipers?

After what felt like an eternity, Raven hung up the receiver. "Okay," she said. "They're waiting for us."

"Who?"

"We've got safe houses all over Berlin. There's one six blocks from here. Just in case anyone makes it over the wall. We're going to have to stay off the main roads, okay?"

"No problem."

"Let's go." Raven led him to the right, down a narrow lane between two industrial buildings. The street was strewn with garbage and discarded metal crates. They turned another corner.

And faced a dead end. A brick wall.

"This is useless," he said.

"Come on. Follow me."

"Follow you where?"

A number of crates had been strategically placed along the wall, allowing Raven and Joshua to clamber up with ease.

They made it over the top. Twenty feet up.

On the other side were similarly strategically placed crates. Just scattered randomly enough that they wouldn't attract attention. But even the most out of shape paper pusher could make it over with ease.

"You guys built this?"

"Yeah. It works better at night. Better than having one of our defectors get shot from a moving car after they've made it across the wall."

They jumped down to street level.

"Only one more block now." They reached the end of the alley. A red Dodge Caravan pulled up on the street ahead of them.

Blocking their escape.

Even from this far distance Joshua could see the driver climb into the back of the vehicle. The side door of the minivan slid open. Revealing a man with a rifle. Raven already had both hands on the pistol stolen from the Russian.

The man aimed.

Raven raised her weapon. Three bursts of gunfire exploded in sonic booms off the walls of the alleyway. One of the Caravan's windows got smashed. The man with the rifle writhed in pain, clutching his arm.

"You're a good shot," said Joshua.

"No, I'm a lucky shot. Let's go back." Raven scampered back up the crates. "I know another way around."

"Why can't we just...."

"Because now they know the route we were headed. If there's one, there'll be more. They'll just phone another car."

"But—"

"We planned for this. Come on."

Joshua shook his head as he followed her up.

89

Joshua bent his knees and jumped. Raven was already ahead of him. Running down the alleyway. Setting a faster pace than the mosey they'd had before.

Things were getting serious.

Joshua got into a jog, close behind. He was now regretting all those long lunches at the CERN cafeteria. It had made him soft. She led him to the right, then to the left. Each alley getting narrower and narrower until they turned onto a path between buildings so tight they had to walk single file. Not a good place to get trapped. Over Raven's shoulder, up ahead Joshua saw it lead to a busy street.

She turned back to him. "Head to the right when you get to the main road."

Joshua was close behind her as the exit to the street became blocked by a figure. Mendel. Barely twenty feet in front of them. At the end of the alley.

He raised his gun. Raven was moving so fast she couldn't—

Mendel's gun discharged.

Raven's chest exploded.

It wouldn't have mattered anyway.

"Get down—" he yelled.

Another shot point blank! In the rib cage. Raven flew backwards.

Joshua dove to the ground. He was so close to Mendel. He flung himself forward.

Another shot went wide.

He tackled Mendel around the knees. Joshua lifted the wiry man up. Slamming him against the walls of the building. The guy grunted on impact. The Uzi he carried fell to the ground. The two of them struggled.

Joshua reached for the gun.

Got it.

Then felt a kick impacting his shins.

Pain.

He dropped the weapon. His leg felt on fire.

Recoiling his right arm, he punched hard. Joshua's fist contacted with Mendel's stomach. A blob of fat and tenderness. The East German fell back, winded. His grip on his gun loosened.

Joshua grabbed the weapon and tossed it as far as possible. It flew onto the sidewalk of the busy street. Skidding under a car. Out of sight.

Joshua stood up. He looked over at Raven.

She was dying.

Anger flooded Joshua's body. "You commie son of a bitch!" He landed a kick to Mendel's face. The German moaned and tried to speak, but could only spit out blood. Damage from the car accident. Must be. He's not going anywhere.

Joshua turned around to Raven. A pool of blood had formed. Her breathing now heavy and rapid. She was about to expire.

Joshua applied CPR. It was no good. She had two giant wounds in her abdomen. The Uzi must be using soft jacket ammo. Exploding on impact.

"You're not going to die on me!" Joshua screamed.

But what the hell was he going to do? She was never going to make it to the hospital. He pumped her heart anyway.

Behind them a car screeched to a halt. A Volkswagen Vanagon. Orange. Bright orange. The door on the side opened. Three dark skinned men in suits burst out. Two of the men grabbed Joshua, dragging him away from Raven.

"No! Let go of me!" He flailed, splattering blood all over their suits.

The third man took a white cloth and a small dark bottle out of his jacket pocket.

As Joshua struggled, he opened the bottle and splashed liquid on the cloth. Then shouted orders at the two men.

One of whom grabbed Joshua by the throat. Held his head.

"She's still alive. You've got to call an ambulance."

The third man pressed the cloth against Joshua's mouth. Held it there. In the far off distance, Joshua heard the sounds of police sirens.

The third man jerked the cloth away. Yelled more orders.

"Don't think you can...."

He looked at Joshua with anger in his eyes. Grabbed the cloth, and nearly forced it down Joshua's throat. He coughed and began to feel dizzy. His vision blurred.

Chloral Hydrate!

The cloth and bottle went away. Joshua felt heavy as the men pulled him into the Vanagon. A seat belt was slapped over his chest.

By the time they got underway he was out cold.

90

When he first became conscious, Joshua couldn't quite open his eyelids. He lay there, still. For minutes? Hours? After a while he noticed his right leg had fallen asleep. Rustling up all his energy, he rolled over. Time passed. He felt his strength returning. His eyelids fluttered.

For a while he just stared at the ceiling, a murky brown tableau.

He was in a room. During the day. It was warm. Afternoon sunlight streamed in. He lifted his head. Sat up. He had been lying on a mat. With a small pillow.

Dressed up in traditional Afghan garb. A grey robe. His head wrapped in some kind of scarf. His feet were bare, but he spotted sandals across the room. At the foot of the mat, blankets had been neatly placed. If the nights got cold.

He looked around. The main room connected with a shower and wash basin. He assumed a squat toilet was in a room adjacent to it. Joshua stood up and touched his skull. Pain. He must be dehydrated. The walls were coated with dark brown plaster. A single lone fan spun above him. The temperature was warm. Nice. Not too hot.

The room was illuminated by a single large window. Some sort of translucent paper had been applied to block the view, giving the space a musty brown hue. Even so, Joshua saw the outline of metal bars. He imagined the door was similarly reinforced. A table occupied one corner of the room, surrounded by cushions. A couple other armchairs took up the space nearby. To the right of the mat five two—liter bottles of water had been lined up. With glasses. On a small side table.

"They thought of everything," he muttered to himself.

He walked toward the door. Tried the handle. Locked. As expected.

On the other side of the room, in the corner, was a thatch container, like a picnic basket. He removed the cover. Inside he found his clothes.

Still stained with Raven's blood.

He shook his head. How had he allowed this to happen? The way things were going, he'd be lucky he wasn't killed.

Under the blood—stained clothes he found his wallet. And his gun belt from Steinberg. The pistol and extra ammo untouched. They must have made a special trip to his hotel room. Just to pick it up. Joshua lifted up the gun and inspected the magazine, below it finding two new ones. They had added to his supply of bullets.

Brave sons of bitches.

He took the gun belt and stuffed the rest of the clothing back. Beside the basket was a pile of books. Maps, some in English. Others in Pashto. Some were professional, for tourists. A couple were manufactured by CIA cartographers with satellite co—ordinates. Others were military battlefield diagrams with the locations of Soviet bases. And a few were hand drawn. Under the maps was a copy of the Koran in English and Arabic.

Joshua grabbed the maps and settled down on his mat. At least this would give him something to do while he waited for whatever was to happen next.

91

The sun slowly crawled towards the horizon. Gradually lowering the light level in the room. To a dim glow. Joshua heard the evening call to prayers in the distance.

The background din he'd grown used to disappeared for a couple of minutes. When it resumed, he guessed he was probably close to a main street. Now at least he knew he was in a city of some kind.

But where?

Feeling tired in the decreasing illumination, he took a nap. But he was woken a few minutes later by the jangle of metal keys in the door. Next came the heavy slam of a metal gate. Joshua woke up from a light doze to a young man approaching with a tray. Dinner by candlelight.

The man sat the tray down by the sleeping mat. He was young. With a large scar running down his right cheek. Despite that, something about him felt out of place in this setting. He seemed too...soft.

"Do you speak English?"

"Yes. My name is Calib. I studied at university in the United States."

"Really? And this was the best job you could get?"

"Some things are worth more than money."

Joshua didn't want to argue with him. At least the guy wasn't trying to get him to convert to Islam. He examined the tray of food. "That smells good. What's for dinner?"

"It's just a simple curry with flatbread. We didn't want to upset your stomach."

"That's very thoughtful of you. Is there any chance I can go see Al—Zawairi tonight?"

"I'm afraid not. My apologies for your accommodation. We've confined you only for your personal safety, and to keep away unwanted attention."

Joshua smiled. "Shall I assume I'm the only white person in the neighborhood?"

Calib grinned meekly. "Tomorrow. Please be patient. I will be back to check in on you every three or four hours. Please remember that this is for your own safety. We don't want you to feel like you are our prisoner."

Joshua eyed the bars on the door. "Perish the thought."

92

In the darkness, and especially in the daytime, Joshua had plenty of time to think. He played the scenario over and over again in his head.

How he was going to kill al—Zawahiri.

He would make small talk. Chit—chat. Once everyone had sat down and relaxed, he would casually pull the gun out and fire. One bullet. Into al—Zawahiri's head.

Of course, it probably meant that Joshua might be killed, too. But it would be worth it. Then there was the issue of François and everyone else working on his return. Part of him thought he owed it to his colleagues to stay alive. So they would know time travel was possible. At least science would benefit. If he died, would they continue to look for him for the rest of their lives? Would such a project even exist if he changed history? Probably. But would he still be working at CERN if he never went to Afghanistan?

Never worked for the CIA? He tried not to think of all the paradoxes. Joshua realized he'd pretty much backed himself into a corner on this one.

He couldn't go back to his normal life. But at the same time, he didn't really want to die. He could be selfish that way.

By the fourth day, Joshua had pretty much given up hope a meeting would happen. As usual he finished his lunch, then took a nap. Once again, after a few minutes Calib interrupted it. This time he entered carrying a tray of tea. It was elaborate. Next to the teapot was a vase of flowers. Real ones. Another Afghani man followed him with some cushions. Joshua hadn't seen him before. The cushions he carried were significantly more luxurious than the ones that furnished the room.

Without a word they set the tea and cushions down. Calib collected Joshua's lunch tray with a nod. The men exited, leaving the door open.

For the first time in days, Joshua got a glimpse of the outside world.

He was in some sort of apartment building. Standing up, he peered outside. The door opened onto a balcony, over a dusty alleyway. From the view of the ground below, it appeared he was on the third floor.

None of this was good. It would make an escape much more difficult than in an ordinary house. Joshua doubted he could jump down without injury. Still, he fingered the pistol under his robe.

No sooner had he reached for the gun than al—Zawahiri appeared. The same as the man Joshua saw captured on CNN, only much less weathered and gray. He had the glasses and thin physique of a doctor. Or a Middle Eastern accountant. The man would not be out of place at a Dungeons and Dragons tournament.

"May I come in?" he said in accented English.

"Of course."

What followed was a series of pleasantries. But when Zawahiri spoke, he talked and talked and talked. Never letting up. Talking about his group's version of the one true Islam. His anger at the Soviet invaders. And his plans for the Afghan resistance. Joshua had no chance to speak.

Somewhere, about twenty minutes into the meeting, Joshua realized he was dealing with a textbook narcissist. A man who believed he was above everyone else. Still, he acted humble and polite, refilling Joshua's tea cup. Even as he berated 'the Marxist infidels.' When the man finally paused, searching for an English word, Joshua asked him how he planned to used the money.

They started to argue with each other. In circles. About what to do with Afghanistan once the Soviets left. It got quite heated.

Finally, al—Zawahiri slammed the table. "I am not the cause of your problems."

"Sure you are. You think you speak for all Muslims."

"I do no such thing. But I believe we are the one true Islam. The others are nothing but pretenders. Margarine Muslims. Unlike you, I do not sacrifice my values to appeal to the masses. I hope the masses will move to me."

"And if they don't, then what? A sarin gas attack here, a truck bomb there?"

"What do you think we're doing with the Soviets? It's all fine when it's for your government."

Joshua was getting angry. He reached into his tunic and pulled out the gun. Al—Zawairi didn't flinch as Joshua flicked off the safety and cocked the weapon. He aimed the gun. No one was in the room with them. No guards. No one to stop him. Neither of them moved.

Time seemed to slow down. Joshua felt himself inhale and exhale. Yet he couldn't pull the trigger.

"Now you see the problem," said al—Zawahiri, almost smugly. "You are a man with something to lose. Indulgence. A life of comfort. A mind of ideas and contradictions. That is what keeps you from shooting."

Joshua lowered his weapon. He couldn't believe he didn't do it. Deep inside, he felt awful.

"Please don't kill me," said al—Zawahiri.

Joshua looked at him. The guy would be responsible for the death of thousands. But he still evoked sympathy.

"Not until I've shown you what we are capable of. Then, if you want, I'll give you another chance."

"Not afraid of anything, are you?"

"I fear imprisonment, but I don't fear death."

93

The day was cold.

Not Chicago winter cold. But a shock to Joshua, who had been walking around in the apartment with a T—shirt the day before. He discovered the building he'd been staying at was in the eastern section of Peshawar. It surprised him to learn he was in Pakistan.

After being dressed up in an obscuring garb, he had left the apartment. Been guided through the streets to a beat up Toyota 4x4. Towing a trailer. With horses inside.

"What is this?" he said to al—Zawahiri.

"We can't drive everywhere."

"How far is it to the border?"

"Forty—five minutes. Then another hour inside Afghanistan. We take the horses after that. A two hour ride to our destination."

"And why are we doing this?"

"I want you to understand fully what we are doing. This will allow that."

"Okay, fine. But what are you planning to show me?"

"Don't worry, I'll let you know when we get there."

He loved to up the suspense, didn't he? thought Joshua.

Getting out of Peshawar was difficult. It had to take quite a bit of patience on behalf of Calib, their driver for the excursion. Joshua sat in the front, chatting with him nonchalantly.

They had packed lots of warm clothing. "Yes," said Calib, "on the other side of the mountains, the climate shifts noticeably."

He was completely right. On the Peshawar side, the temperature would be considered almost summer weather in central Europe. They drove into a narrow mountain pass. Was this the Khyber? The place that would later be bombed to shreds by the Americans? In less than fourteen years in the future? They passed the almost—non—existent border check, in the city of Torkham. Now well past the mountain ranges, the temperature had dropped at least fifteen degrees Celsius. The cold breeze made Joshua put up his window.

The roads were terrible. Not a bit of asphalt. Just dust. After an hour's drive across a plateau, Joshua began to recognize landmarks. He knew this route. Or at least, someday he would. From the mountains it was about a four hour journey to Kabul. If the road wasn't obstructed, which it often was. And yet, so far on the journey, they hadn't encountered anyone at all. Certainly not any Soviets. They turned off a side road, continuing for another half an hour. Until they reached a gully, not passable by car.

Calib slowed down.

Al—Zawairi and Joshua got out. Joshua scanned the horizon. They were at the top of a cliff. Beyond which lie a wide plateau. Off to his left. Ending in a far off mountain range. They were close to some jagged hills. Clearly a perfect hiding place.

"Here," said Calib, "keep your door closed. I don't want the sand to get in. These winds, they kick up dust easily."

"You also," said al—Zawairi to Joshua, "want to get dressed. Take some of the garments we brought. It's cold."

Joshua put on gloves and a knit cap. And added a layer of vests. At the back of the trailer, Calib wrangled the horses. Got some supplies ready. Joshua followed as al—Zawairi approached the edge of the cliff. They looked out at the horizon, stretching out over hundreds of miles.

"From here we go on horseback. These hills are one of the only things keeping the Russians out of Pakistan."

"How long will it take?"

"Have you ever ridden a horse?"

"A few times."

Al—Zawairi laughed.

For the next forty—five minutes the two of them rode through the flat brush lands. Almost a desert, so sparse was the vegetation. Into the hills. Once in the rocks, they began to climb. At first Joshua found it a struggle to get his horse up the mountain. Of the two animals, Joshua's was less interested in heading upwards.

After a couple of hours climbing the hills, they stopped at a rocky outcrop. Al—Zawahiri dismounted. Tied up his horse. And opened a leather pouch. He'd brought lunch for the two of them. Flatbreads and lamb kebab.

Joshua snuck away under the pretense to take a piss. Once out of sight, he checked his gun. He would make damn sure this guy wasn't getting out alive.

One thing was for sure. Al—Zawahiri was certainly brave for taking him here. It had crossed Joshua's mind he was being led into a trap. But to what ends? These people needed money. This was all song and dance.

After feeding the horses, they resumed their journey deeper into the hills. Half an hour later they entered a narrow gulley. It got so tight they had to dismount. At the end of it they reached the side of a cliff. A narrow path with a sheer drop—off of hundreds of feet. Barely wide enough for the horses. Should they get frightened, it could be the end of them all. The trail led into what looked like a cave.

"Do we keep going?"

"Yes," said al—Zawahiri, his voice echoing off the walls. "Trust me."

Joshua felt around for his pistol. Should he kill him now? But the horses...if they bolted, they might stampede over both of them. Then there was the sheer curiosity of where they were going.

They turned a corner and darkness closed in.

94

The sunlight reappeared a minute later.

Getting closer, the exit of the tunnel emerged onto another cliff. But this time it was quite spacious. With more than enough room to set up camp, for several people.

Al—Zawahiri beckoned.

Joshua got off his horse and handed the reins over. Somebody had built a post to tie up horses. Al—Zawahiri knew what he was doing. Like he'd been here several times before.

Joshua wandered around the site. Off to the left he found a path through the wall of rock, smooth enough that it could have been cut through by a machine.

He decided to follow it.

The walls of rock were about twelve feet high on either side, like a trench. Following the corridor another fifty feet or so, Joshua turned his body sideways. Such was the degree the path narrowed. Good thing he wasn't obese. At one point he had to almost squeeze through a bit of outcrop before the path widened again. He kept going, and the trail ended at a small open area. With several other paths leading off. He looked over at the one closest to his right. It led to a large cave. The opening was wide enough to make the cavern well—lit.

Joshua took a few steps in.

Not much here, he thought. But it would be a good place to hide. No bats, at least. He turned a corner and the cave dropped down, into darkness. For all Joshua knew, it might go deep into the mountain. The whole place could be like a maze.

Satisfied there wasn't anyone hiding along the other paths, he moved back to the main clearing.

Al—Zawairi was busy feeding the horses with oats he brought in.

"Is this what your brought me to see? A bunch of caves?"

Al—Zawahiri smiled and shook his head. "I promised I wouldn't disappoint." He beckoned to the right.

A small path led off around the side of the cliff. Wide enough to walk comfortably, without worrying about falling off. It was a long way down. The floor of the valley was at least several hundred feet below. They turned a corner and the trail widened out to a large space. Wider than where they left the horses.

But Joshua had barely noticed it. He couldn't stop looking at the landscape below—

An enormous Soviet air base.

"Stunning, isn't it?" said al—Zawahiri.

"Not exactly prime real estate."

The landing strip was gigantic. Surrounded by near identical buildings. Lined up row after row, vehicles buzzing around them. It stretched on for miles. "They must bring everything in from Kabul—fuel, water, rations. They're bleeding their treasuries pretending to be kings."

Joshua was distracted by a noise from the sky. An airplane approached. An Antonov cargo jet buzzed over their heads. Almost too close. But it was the color that burned into his mind.

The plane was painted orange. Neon pink and bright orange.

"What the hell?" muttered Joshua.

"We're going to have front row seats."

The plane circled around the valley and began its approach. It was a gigantic airplane. One of the Antonov models was the largest plane ever built to carry cargo and passengers. Joshua was terrible at identifying aircraft. The pilot flew the plane as if he was some sort of daredevil, swooping down after he had finished a full 360 around the base. Like he was landing in the Alaska bush. Except the plane had six jet engines.

379

Some kind of horn sounded from the hills below. Al—Zawairi passed him a pair of binoculars. "You might want these."

Joshua took them. Followed the plane as it landed and taxied in.

Then the air craft exploded.

The tarmac in front of the plane erupted in a ball of flames. Then he saw tail fire from a projectile emanating from the valley below. Hit the cockpit of the plane, on target. The front of the aircraft exploded.

Moments later more rockets fired, destroying the rest of the plane's fuselage.

95

Joshua stood frozen, overwhelmed by a mixture of terror and awe. Yet another rocket had fired from the hills below. Hitting the rear of the plane. The fuselage was now nothing more than a hulk of black flames and smoke. Emergency crews from the air base raced towards the fire. Even from the faraway distance of the cliff it was clear that looking for survivors would be hopeless.

"There were four hundred Soviet troops on that aircraft."

Things got stranger. On the tarmac a line of tanks had appeared. They were heading to the edge of the air base. Towards Joshua and al—Zawahiri.

In the desert below dozens of figures emerged out of the dirt. Carrying RPG weapons. They ran back towards the mountains, but the tanks moved quickly over the terrain. Some of them, instead of running, turned around and began firing at the Soviets. It was a full—on battle as the tanks returned fire.

A second line of Mujahideen appeared, much closer. Firing from the hills just below Joshua and al—Zawahiri. The cliffside echoed with mortar fire. Now that took balls, thought Joshua, with your battle lines backed up against the hills. Those weren't guns you could move quickly. Most came in on the back of a truck. The fighters were outfitted like it was the Second World War going on down there.

And the Soviets...how had they let the insurgents get so close? Were they really that incompetent? To have such enemies on their doorstep? Maybe there were good reasons why they had lost this war.

A blast from the tank tore into the cliffs below. Al—Zawahiri winced. "We should go back to the horses. It isn't safe here."

"Damn right it isn't."

At the campsite Joshua circled around, looking to see if anyone from the group of fighters below was about to appear. "Do you think we can make it back before dark?"

"I'm not sure. Either way, I have many friends in these parts."

"I don't doubt it."

Al—Zawairi pulled some seeds out of his pocket to feed one of the horses. "To a man like you, all of this must look primitive. Horses. Caves. But we have the one thing that the Russians cannot buy—the will to win." He smiled and stroked the horse's mane. "After all you've seen, can you really kill me?"

Joshua replied with a bullet!

The handgun cracked through the air. The horses bolted upward, nearly breaking free of their reins. Al—Zawairi ran away, in the direction of the air base, blood streaming down his right calf.

Joshua cocked his weapon. And fired again.

The next bullet hit al—Zawairi in the left thigh. He collapsed to the ground, writhing in pain. A thigh bone damaged by gunfire is probably one of the most painful injuries a human body can suffer. However, as Joshua knew full well, it wasn't anywhere near fatal.

He walked over slowly to al—Zawahiri, watching the man sobbing like a baby. Had it all come to this? A man who had once been a doctor, now terrified by pain?

Al—Zawairi turned around to face the man who attacked him. "What are you? Some kind of Russian?"

"No." Joshua stayed stone—faced as he raised his pistol. He felt nothing.

Another shot erupted.

Except—

Joshua hadn't fired. He ducked down.

Someone else was shooting at him from the entrance.

96

Joshua dove toward the horses. Undid their ties. The animals bolted. Creating a distraction as Joshua made a run for the caves. His heart raced. He wouldn't last long running. This route might only lead to dead ends. And whoever was shooting at him might know that. Sure, he could go into the caves, but he didn't have a flashlight.

He was screwed either way.

How could one of al—Zawahiri's men be shooting at him? Wouldn't Joshua have seen them come up from the valley below? The rock next to Joshua's head exploded. He ducked down, but didn't see anyone behind him. He moved to the side. Kept going. Emerged where the path split.

There was still the pistol. He just hoped there wasn't more than one fighter pursuing him. There weren't enough bullets in his magazine.

This is crazy. He grabbed his gun and crouched

down by the end of the gully. Using the rocks as cover.

He saw a figure appear at the far end of the path. At first hard to distinguish in the mid—afternoon shadows. A man wearing desert army camouflage. Brown and tan patterns. Typical issue for this environment. This individual wasn't with al—Zawahiri. The figure got closer.

It was MacLean. Carrying a 12—gauge shotgun.

Good god, what was he trying to do?

Joshua watched as MacLean reloaded. The shotgun was far from a practical weapon. That's why Joshua had been able to get this far. He watched as MacLean fumbled with the shells.

"What the hell do you want, Major?"

MacLean stood still, as if hit by an electric shock. He didn't like being watched. "You know what I want. I've come to get you and—"

"We're on the same side, you idiot!"

MacLean finished loading his shotgun. "Don't you try to pull the wool over my eyes, boy. I know you're some kind of Ruskie trying to take down the rest of us. The whole operation."

He saw MacLean glance down at the ground. Like he'd discovered something useful. Joshua followed his gaze.

Blood.

He reached over to his upper left arm. He was wounded and dripping all over. For Christ's sake, he hadn't even felt it. Joshua looked around for an escape.

The cave.

He raised his gun in MacLean's direction, not bothering to aim. Fired off three shots.

While MacLean ducked and covered in the gully, Joshua made a run for the cave. A moment passed before MacLean realized Joshua wasn't going to charge him. MacLean bolted up and dashed to the side of the gully. For all he knew, Joshua was out of bullets.

With his back against the rock wall, MacLean moved sideways, getting closer to the end where the paths split.

He raised his shotgun.

And saw a trail of blood on the ground below him.

What the hell?

The line of blood split up, in two directions.

One towards another gully. The other towards a cave. Had Joshua considered him so stupid that he'd take the wrong path? The trail of blood heading off to the gully was twice as thick.

Which meant only one thing. He now knew Joshua was hiding in the cave.

MacLean smiled. I've got you now, buddy.

97

MacLean had been fighting off jetlag all day. Waiting for this asshole. His body's circuitry felt like it had been completely fried. He did not want to face a long, drawn—out standoff. At the edge of a cave. He wanted this guy out of here. Whether it meant the target was dead or alive. He wasn't going to risk his own life, not with half an army of Afghan resistance fighters on their way here.

He yawned.

Normally, he'd be waking up right about now.

Joshua, meanwhile, sat well inside the cavern, more wide awake than he'd been in days. Hiding behind a rock. He saw MacLean's figure silhouetted in the entrance.

Shafts of light peeked through, highlighting Joshua's face. MacLean couldn't see him. Yet. But they were a lot closer than MacLean knew.

"Hey, listen," said MacLean. "You've got to come out of there. I don't want to hurt you. There's only me. We'll go back to the States. I'll keep you away from the boys out here—"

"Why are you doing this?"

"We all thought you might be some whacko Ruskie agent, but I think you might just have been brainwashed, or—"

"Are you fucking crazy?"

MacLean was taken aback. He didn't like that kind of language. Especially from young people. This guy must be some kind of crazy hippy. Or worse. He should have known better, trusting someone with sideburns like that. "Now, you listen here, son. I don't predict the future. For all I know it will be another hundred years before we defeat the Soviets—"

"You people are totally clueless. Two years from now the Berlin Wall will collapse. By 1991 the Soviet Union will cease to exist. You've already won, and you can't even...."

A shotgun shell exploded near the roof of the cave. Sand and rocks rained down on Joshua.

"You crazy mother—"

MacLean had enough of this insanity. This guy was fucking up a major tactical operation against Soviet forces. This wasn't going to end well if he tried to negotiate. The only way would be to take him out before he could do more damage. And al—Zawahiri had to get to a hospital. They didn't have time to pussy around with Joshua.

"I am not going to let this situation get out of control. You've got to the count of three or you're coming home in a black bag. Three...."

MacLean moved in closer.

"Two...."

Joshua closed his eyes. Waiting for the shotgun blast.

"One."

Nothing.

MacLean looked around awkwardly. Joshua wasn't moving. The bluff was being called. MacLean didn't want to kill.

"You Commie son—of—a—bitch, you asked for it!"

MacLean raised the shotgun.

And the cave exploded in blue lightening.

Small sonic booms echoed off the walls of the cave. MacLean clutched at his ears.

The lighting disappeared. MacLean's hands were shaking. What the bejesus was that? He reached into his right pants pocket and grabbed a powerful flashlight. Switching it on, he followed the trail of blood.

He went deeper into the cave.

And deeper.

Behind a rock. Until the trail disappeared. Raising his flashlight, MacLean followed the curves of the wall. Until he realized he was at a dead end.

There was no way out, except past him.

98

At first Joshua didn't understand why Axel and François looked so concerned.

Then he saw the blood pooling at his feet. After that came a rush of light—headedness. He dropped to his knees, clutching at his arm. Then lay down on his side. He wanted to take a nap.

Blood was everywhere. MacLean's shotgun had been more effective than he'd thought.

Joshua looked to the other side of The Gulag. Through the white webbing. François and the older Axel rushed down the steps to the floor of the reactor.

"Is he alive?" asked François.

"Careful," said Axel. "He might be injured. Keep pressure on that wound."

Joshua began to stir. "Don't worry," he said. "It's just a flesh wound. Nothing serious."

"What the hell were you doing?" asked Axel.

"Hiding out in a cave."

"The doctor will be here any minute," said François.

"Just tell me what year it is."

François smiled and clasped Joshua's hand.

99

The mood in the operating room was relaxed. Dr. Foote had been brought in from the U.S. Army hospital in Landstuhl. Few surgeons in the world had more experience removing bullets. Or understanding when it was important not to remove them.

Joshua had been anesthetized. There were several other doctors around the table, assisting. Monitoring his vital signs. Joshua was completely covered with green smocks. Except for a small patch of skin around a bullet hole, covered with iodine.

The surgeon inserted a long, thin clamp into the tiny round wound. The other doctors had their eyes on a monitor, showing the position of the clamp in the body. They had a new kind of imaging sensor that gave a translucent overlay of other organs near the camera. A second monitor gave a realtime display of where the clamps were in the body. This was only the fourth time this technology had ever been used.

One of the doctors toggled a control. An overlay of a CT scan taken half an hour earlier appeared. It would be their map to the bullet.

The projectile itself hadn't done all that much damage. But it had penetrated through the abdominal cavity, creating vacuoles of air. It had sealed when the blood had clotted, but the cavity was now septic.

Dangerous bacteria was now growing on Joshua's insides.

The tissue that had narcotized around the bullet path would have to be cut away and the remaining areas washed. Then sewn up. He was lucky it had only hit his small intestine. And nothing worse, like the spinal cord. Doctor Foote was careful. Made sure he didn't scratch anything on the way. After twenty minutes, the clamp retracted, holding the remains of a bullet.

The surgeon placed it in a small metal bowl.

The next day, as Joshua was recovering, Axel's assistant placed the remains of the bullet in a brace, just like the Lego astronaut at the beginning of these experiments in the hadron collider.

Right in the path of the electron beam. Once they were powered up, a blue beam hit the remains of the metal shard.

In the control room Axel and François watched the results from the experiment appear on different monitors. There were graphs. Lines of sensor readings. And pie charts.

For the rest of the day they went over the data carefully. Meticulously. Well into the night. But in the end François looked over at Axel and shook his head. "We've learned nothing from this."

100

Never in his wildest dreams had Joshua imagined that so many people he knew could afford to send him flowers.

The room overflowed with them. Every surface covered with a vase or bouquet. Or get well cards. There was almost no space to sit down in the small Geneva hospital room.

It had been a long week since his surgery. Finally François had found a moment to come and visit him. Perhaps there had been a certain degree of trepidation. Maybe he didn't want to disturb Joshua. The doctors wanted him to keep still while the wounds healed. But it made Joshua suspect that François didn't have good news for him.

François had arrived about an hour earlier. He didn't bring flowers, but had been kind enough to sneak in a print edition of a Playboy magazine. And some hash brownies. Probably not a good idea, but the doctors had said he could go back on solid food.

For the past half hour they'd been discussing what had happened in the collider. "So," said François, "on the final attempt we decided to let the radiation levels go far beyond the red line. We even overloaded a couple of the collimators."

"And what did you make of it?"

"I don't know how we're going to recreate the circumstance of your disappearance."

"My 'disappearance'?" Joshua had made a report about everything that had happened. Why were they using such misnomers?

"That's what it's being called," said François.

"But we've been over this. I went back in time."

François reclined in his chair and sighed. "Just because you saw something, doesn't mean it's there. Like a mirage, in the desert."

Joshua scowled. "Excuse me?"

"We've had someone look into your story. The only thing we can confirm is that the Knicks did lose on Friday the thirteenth in 1987. Axel, for one, would have remembered you."

Joshua leaned over, as if he wanted to shake some sense into François, but a wave of pain held him back. "I don't understand."

"Easy there, Monsieur. I have an idea, but it's pretty out there."

"Unlike what I've been through?" Why was he so aggressive? Probably all the drugs pumping through his body.

"I don't think you traveled back in time. I think you slid sideways into a parallel universe. Perhaps their laws of physics work differently than ours, but the difference would be so small as to be almost undetectable."

"Okay."

"So time might flow faster in our universe, just enough to make their 1987 occur thirty years behind ours."

"But the people, the events—"

"It's a hypothesis. God knows how we'd ever test it."

With that, Joshua felt deflated. "Yeah."

"Anyway, I've got to get back to the control room. Lots more work to finish up."

Joshua lay back. "You did well. To come up with a solution in six weeks was amazing."

François looked at him, concern in his eyes.

"What?" said Joshua, not understanding.

"You spent how long in 1987?"

"I told you. Six weeks." Joshua knew something was up. "What? How much time has passed here? I thought it was only a week. It was only a week, right?"

"No."

"How long?"

"Two and a half years."

Joshua closed his eyes.

"I should go," said François.

Joshua sat up. "It's okay, I just want to...."

"Don't worry. I'll come back tomorrow." François got up to leave.

"Thanks for coming by."

"No problem."

He was on his way out when he turned around. "Oh, and there's some woman from the American consulate wanting to see you. She came around yesterday."

"To interrogate me?"

"She's pretty hot. I'd let her tie me up and play twenty questions."

101

His nap was shattered by the click of high heels. Echoing through the room. It was the day after François' visit. Joshua opened his eyes slowly. A nurse was looking him over. "There's a visitor who wants to see you, but I told her—"

"It's okay. I'm awake."

The nurse beckoned to someone just outside the door. His blood pressure skyrocketed when he saw who it was. At first he couldn't believe his eyes.

He was looking at Raven.

Shock registered on Joshua's face. The woman stopped mid—stride. She was surprised by his reaction. "Hello, Mr. Sinclair. My name is Ruby Fairweather."

Ruby took a card out of her purse. Joshua realized something was different about this woman. The hair. The nose. Could this be Raven's daughter?

Ruby handed her card to Joshua. A government card. With the seal of the State Department. "I'm from the consulate in Geneva. If now's a bad time, I could come back later."

Emotion welled up behind Joshua's eyes. "Now is fine."

"Thank you." Ruby sat down. Pulled out a clipboard with official looking note paper. "I have a few questions I'd like to ask."

Joshua looked over the woman. "Is your mother still alive?"

Ruby didn't know what to say. She wasn't expecting this. "Actually, my mother died when I was a child. In...."

"1987," finished Joshua. "In West Berlin."

"Um, yes."

"She was shot twice. In the heart and in the stomach by a Soviet agent."

Ruby was taken aback. Part of her wanted to flee. Something was seriously wrong here. "Who told you that? Nobody knows that. How did you—"

Joshua took her hand. "This is going to take some time to explain."

Don't miss the next chapter in The Counter Clock Trilogy!

The Nagasaki Project

Turn the page for a preview of
The Nagasaki Project...

The swastika armband was too tight.

Akira Fujimoto had picked it up in the Sapporo Tanukiko-ji—the covered pedestrian shopping street in the heart of Suskino. At a store that specialized in historic costumes, comic books and role playing games. Sato—san had sent him up there. To courier several kilograms of amphetamine salts back to Tokyo, that had been shipped from Russia via the port at Wakkanai.

While waiting for the drugs to arrive, Akira had spent a day and a half wandering the largest city on the island of Hokkaido. Some of Sato—san's associates there had taken him out for drinks, and then later had sent a girl from the local delivery health provider to his room for oral sex and other services.

The next day, severely hung over, he'd wandered the Tanukikoji, stopping in at shoe stores and haberdasheries. But it was the Nazi uniform in the window that had enticed him into the comic book store. He hadn't wanted the uniform, but the armband appealed to him. The bright red would look good against his black leather jacket. It would also be useful to strike fear into the less savory characters he encountered on his work for Sato—san.

Tonight he would need to instill that fear.

Since then, Akira had never been back to Sapporo. He almost never left Tokyo. Even a trip to Shonan or Chiba had become a rare occurrence for him. He was just too busy. It wasn't like he was some low level street tout, directing customers to a massage parlor. He was a leader. A man with responsibilities. Someone had to make sure these business owners paid up. And on time. That was always the problem, wasn't it? Sure, they wanted the protection of the local yakuza. But no one wanted to pay up.

Akira looked in the mirror, combing back his hair. His apartment was small, no more than six and a half tatami mats. But it suited him fine, for now. Hikari wanted him to move in with her. But he valued his freedom.

He put the comb down and examined his face. A straight horizontal wrinkle had appeared across his forehead. This was new.

He grabbed a bandanna hanging on the metal rack he used to dry his futon in winter. Wrapped it around his skull to hide the wrinkle. The perfect image of an American biker. Like

Marlon Brando in The Wild One.

But still...Akira would never be a high level yakuza. He didn't have the family connections. Or the ruthlessness. He had heard stories. Like the factions in Kyushu. Now there was a rough bunch of gangsters. Killing the leader and his mistress. They'd found a way to get a promotion. Akira just didn't have it in him. He didn't mind his work—it was better than sweating it out in a Saitama auto parts factory. Or working the graveyard shift at Seven—Eleven, waiting for someone to come in and negotiate for the cash register at knifepoint.

No, he'd never own a hostess bar. Have access to all those beautiful women. Be their boss. Maybe even arrange a favor or two from them. Of course, there was also the fact that he'd never have to worry about going into debt with the wrong people. Or that his head might end up in a cabbage patch somewhere on the outskirts of Kumagaya.

He stood up and moved over to his clothing rack. The last thing he needed to do was prepare the duffel bag. He unzipped it, realizing it was still filled with two large brown bags of cash. You could buy a pretty nice car with that amount of money. Pulling over a chair and climbing on top of it, he pushed one of the asbestos ceiling panels out of the way. It was hardly a fool—proof location, but it would stop a casual thief. Of all Tokyo's twenty—three special wards, Taito Ward currently had the worst reputation for break—ins.

Once the cash was stashed, he filled the duffel bag with a dress shirt, necktie, and navy dress pants he'd purchased at Uniqlo. Along with extra socks, underwear, and dental floss. Then headed out.

Akira's apartment was on the second floor of a concrete apartment building. Unique on this block. He shut his door and walked down the hallway. The corridor was exposed to the elements, as was the stairwell. Not uncommon in the Kanto region, as there was little chance of blowing snow, even in winter. The building stood in the midst of several older, tightly—packed wooden buildings, many with traditional balconies. Several of the local news magazines considered neighborhoods like this the most dangerous in Tokyo. Not just for the crime—should a major earthquake strike nearby, there was a very real danger of these buildings catching fire, an almost inevitable result of a major quake. Some of the structures were over fifty years old, which made them kindling in the off—chance of a conflagration.

Akira lived a ten—minute walk from Minami—Senju station. Not far enough from the stink of the Tokyo Water Reclamation plant, but close enough to the soaplands and love hotels of Yoshiwara.

Underneath the second floor was a covered parking area. Most people didn't want to live on the first floor, especially women—too much chance of a Peeping Tom. So many build-ers had elected to turn the ground floor into open spaces for cars and motorcycles. Akria was happy he didn't pay extra to park his bike, a Kawasaki ZZ—R1100 with a 750cc engine. He had spent plenty of money to get the special license needed to drive these more powerful motorcycles. Packing the duffel bag on the back compartment, he started the bike.

As the engine roared away, he thought about the tasks that lay ahead of him. Tonight there would be trouble with foreigners.

2

The entire crowd was Filipino nannies. They worked for rich white people who lived in Roppongi and Hiro—o. Imported because, unlike almost all Japanese, they spoke fluent English. And they worked cheap. Most stayed a year or two, remitting back funds to their families. Some even used it as a springboard for immigrating to Canada or the United States.

Monday was their usual day off. They gathered weekly at this Catholic church in Azabu—Juuban. There was a five o'clock mass in Tagalog. It was one of the few churches in Tokyo, and probably the only one with a basement. Certainly some women came for the religion, but mostly for the free food, and the chance to compare notes on their employers.

The one downside was that the priest always screened a movie before the dinner reception. One with a religious theme, usually some dramatization of a biblical story. And always on an old 16mm film print. With terrible sound. The church was too cheap to invest in a modern video projection system.

The film print was faded a dusky orange color, so often had it been screened. Jesus had walked into a small village, and was being questioned by the local elders. Then a woman led him to the dead body of Lazurus.

Everyone in the film, from Jesus down to the extras in the background, was Japanese. The dialog was also in Japanese, with Chinese subtitles. Some of the women whispered softly to each other, explaining the narrative for those who were confused.

Standing by the projector, waiting to change reels, stood Father Santos. He too, was Filipino. A Catholic priest from Laguna. Probably the only person in the Tokyo Diocese who still knew how to work the old Elmo projector. He felt bad for these women—despite living in a first world city, many of them bunked four to a room in order to save money. And none of them were young, mostly middle—aged or older. The choice between taking a job overseas or staying stuck in rural poverty.

On the screen, Japanese Jesus had just brought Lazurus back to life. The village people waved palms all around him, celebrating the miracle. Some of the people in the crowd on the screen asked who Jesus was. Father Santos remembered that the filmmakers had gotten the story all wrong—the resurrection of Lazurus had taken place before, not after, Jesus was crucified by the Romans. Oh, well, he thought, he'd have to explain this once the film was over.

Of course, Father Santos didn't know that he'd get no such chance. Akira was on his way.

3

He cruised his bike down Showa Dori, the main route from Minami—Senju into central Tokyo. Akira passed Ueno Station, then on past the bright lights of Okachimachi. He was tempted to stop and meet his favorite masseuse, but then quashed the idea. Naoto and the gang were waiting at a Lawson parking lot near Kinshicho Station. First they had to deal with the ramen cook. It couldn't wait any longer. He had to be spoken to tonight, or Sato—san would get on Akira's case.

At least the temperature wasn't cold. They would get their tasks done quickly. He could make it to Hikari's apartment by nine o'clock, in time for dinner. As he'd promised.

Akira turned his bike east. It was almost time to wreck havoc.

4

The Lawson convenience store was just behind the Sumo stables midway between Kinshicho and Ryogoku. Everyone was already there. Naoto, Akira's second—in—command, was dressed in his usual bright yellow crash leather. They always chose this location because the parking lot was frequently empty, even this early in the evening.

Akira pulled up, hopped off his bike, and lit up a cigarette. There were five of them in the group tonight—an indication their tasks ahead would be important. Usually it was just him and Naoto doing the rounds. Extra muscle meant that Sato—san was taking the rental situation pretty damn seriously.

"So," said Akira. "You know we only have two stops tonight?"

Naoto nodded. "These foreigners, can any of them speak Japanese?"

"Probably not. But we'll scream at them anyway. They should get the message if we're loud enough." Akira took his cigarette and stubbed it out in the mailbox—sized ashtray next to the convenience store's recycling bins. "I need to be in Setagaya by nine o'clock."

"Why? No time for drinks?" said Naoto. "Your girlfriend has you whipped."

"Hey," said Akira puffing up his chest, pushing himself in Naoto's way, like a tough guy. Then he made a mock—swipe with his fist.

"Fine," said Naoto. "We'll work quickly. But we've got to move."

Akira turned towards his bike. "Come on, everybody, let's go."

"But first," said Naoto, "we have to show them how to get there."

Akira looked over at the three goons they'd picked up for the night. "Fine." He produced a map from his coat pocket. Instructed the thugs on the exact route they'd take through the city. The Tokyo metropolis was terrible to navigate through. Two of the bikers had joined them from Shonan in Kanagawa, and the third had come in from some butt—fuck nowhere town up in the north of Saitama. As Akira explained where they were going, it became clear to him that these young grunts would never be able to find their way around. So, in the end, he told them just to keep an eye on Naoto's yellow jacket. Akira told him to load them out.

Naoto got on his bike, muttering about the nine o'clock deadline. What a whiner, thought Akira. The guy was always complaining. He could never take the lead, could he? But worse, and this point was in agreement amongst most people in the organization, Naoto was stupid. Making him pretty much the opposite of Akira. Without brains, how else could one successfully live a double life?

5

The bikes roared out of the parking lot. Probably much to the chagrin of people living in the nearby apartment blocks. But they knew it was pointless to complain about the bousou-zoku.

Naoto took the lead. As he turned onto the road, he hit the far right lip of the curb where it sloped upwards. His bike wobbled as he regained control.

Unbelievable, thought Akira, he's so incompetent. How many years has he been riding a motorcycle? And Akira, alone amongst tonight's group, had an engine over 750 cc. After all this time, Naoto still hadn't passed the driver's test for the larger motorcycle engines.

They followed the roads that paralleled the Chuo Line. At Kinshicho station they headed south, towards the Shitoko. Passing love hotels nestled under the expressway. Turning onto a narrow street, they found the ramen shop, their first destination of the night. Akira needed to have a conversation with the owner.

They burst through the doors. "Look at this," said Akira.

Two customers, finishing up their bowls of noodles and broth, cowered in the corner.

An old man appeared from behind the counter. Skinny, balding and short. The man had owned the shop for decades. But he hadn't been paying his protection money for months. Akira couldn't understand these people at all. Who did they expect to save them if they were threatened by another faction? What if someone walked in here, from a rival yakuza gang, and smashed their hands on one of the glass bowls? Pretended they were injured? Made it a public embarrass-ment for the owner? Where would the guy be then? That's how many of the factions operated, moving in on new turf. The yakuza thug would make the whole incident a big deal—police phoned, newspapers called—all to get the guy to pay up. It would be a mess. Without the protection of the Yamaguchi—gumi, and their lay soldiers, like Akira.

Of course, everyone understood the economy was bad. But the ramen shop owner had made no attempt to settle his backlog of payments. That, however, was no excuse.

Naoto and the three goons dragged the owner up off his feet.

"In the back," said Akira.

"But wait," said the old man, "I'm sorry I didn't have the money—"

Akira smiled. "This is no time for excuses."

The ramen shop owner shook his head. "I'll go bankrupt. My landlord...my business has been terrible."

Akira motioned to the thugs. "The pants. Get the pants down."

The goon from Saitama untied the old man's white cooking apron. After that he unzipped the jeans underneath, ripping them down with the underwear. The old man's crotch was exposed.

"Down on the ground," said Akira. "Get him down."

One of the Shonan thugs emerged from a back storage room carrying a giant plastic jar of mustard. At least four or five liters. He unscrewed the giant lid.

Akira took the open bottle and poured it on the old man's crotch. Mustard glooped all over the man's genitalia and stomach. Then Akira leaned down and slapped the old man. "So you better pay up," he said. "Or we'll be back in two weeks. It would be a shame for this place to burn down, wouldn't it?"

The thugs all laughed at that.

Akira motioned to the exit. "Let's go. It's time to deal with the foreigners."

6

The modernist cathedral crammed itself in between high—end Azabu—Juuban apartment towers. In the basement, the Jesus movie was still playing, almost over.

Many of the Filipino women were asleep. Others sat up, awake but looking bored. A few talked in whispers at the back. Japanese Jesus was being applauded by the townsfolk. Then lifted up onto a donkey by a group of men in robes, the colors of which had muddled into shades of brown and tan by the faded film print. The peasants rejoiced with adulation.

Japanese Jesus was saved. Heading off towards the sunset.

Almost on cue, Akira and the bousouzoku gang burst through the doors to the church hall. The two thugs from Shonan swung metal chains around, swooping down. The women in the front retracted their feet in terror as the chain impacted the metal legs of the cheap folding chairs. It made an ungodly racket.

Akira stood up front, the end of the movie projecting over his figure. "Everybody!"

A woman in the front row screamed.

"Calm down," said Akira in Japanese. He turned to Naoto.

"Shut down that projector."

Naoto walked over to the old Elmo. Puzzled by the antiquated piece of technology, he reached down and ripped out the power cord. One of the other thugs flicked on the overhead fluorescents.

Akira had left his sunglasses on to look extra frightening to the women. "So," he screamed, "some of you have been very, very late paying your rent. Thinking you have the protection of the law behind you. And that is very true. Your landlords cannot compel the police to rip you out of your lodgings. But we—" he indicated to Naoto and the thugs who moved up behind him— "are not the police. Nor do we follow their laws. I'm not going to pick out those who are transgressing, as surely you will just rally around and protect each other." Akira strode past the front row of seats. "Consider yourselves lucky we're not calling the immigration services on you. We are the only thing between some of you and the authorities who would see you deported. So you better keep that in mind if you don't pay your rent."

A woman with long hair in the front row began to scream at Akira in Tagalog.

"You stupid foreigner," said Akira, "be quiet."

She belted out another scream in anger, ran up and pounded her fists against Akira's chest. He threw her down against the floor.

"Hey," yelled an obese middle—aged women who had been sitting nearby, "how dare you do that—"

"Oh, yeah?" said Akira. He leaned forward and slapped the woman hard, drawing blood from her lip. The entire crowd started screaming in panic. "What? Is there something you wanted to say to me?"

The woman mumbled something in English.

Akira growled. "I said say it in Japanese."

"I sorry, so sorry," said the obese woman in Japanese.

"Say it correctly."

The woman started crying, blubbering all over the place. Akira could barely make her out. "Don't no hit again," she finally managed to blurt out.

Akira shook his head. She had gotten the verb ending wrong. No respect for him at all, was there? It seemed the woman only spoke Japanese in the casual register, like a child.

Again, she looked up at him, tears streaming down her cheeks. "I'm sorry, please do not hit me again."

Akira smiled. "When you say it like that, of course I won't." He gestured to the crowd. "All of you had better listen up. You ought to take care, in the manner in which you address your landlords. Or even those representatives who collect the rent. Appropriate for you, who are guests in our country. I know several of you have been paying late this last month. This is a warning to let you know we will visit you in person, if need be."

"Stop," came the voice in English. The priest appeared at the back. Father Santos. He switched to Japanese. "That's enough." He walked right up to Akira, stopping mere inches from his face. Uncomfortably close. "Get out. Your message is clear. There was no need to hit her."

Akira narrowed his gaze. The priest, who he presumed was also Filipino, spoke flawless Japanese.

But Father Santos didn't back down. "I'm surprised to see you. The bousouzoku dealing with foreigners. I didn't know they let your type represent Japan. The scum of the yakuza. Visiting foreign churches. That's a new one, isn't it? Your type isn't exactly known for its subtlety."

Akira hissed. "They don't pay their rent."

The priest didn't back down. "What kind of trash like you comes into a place of worship? Go back to Shitamachi and leave us alone."

Akira grabbed him by the lapels and slammed him back down against the concrete floor.

A woman nearby screamed.

Akira kicked the priest in the chest. He stopped when he saw the blood pooling by Father Santos's head.

The women in the audience stood up. One started yelling in Tagalog. Another woman got out her phone. Others started to scream.

Akira felt his body flooded with panic. His sunglasses had fallen off. As he picked them up, he realized he would be recognized by the women. Blood from the priest's skull had splattered on the lenses. He wiped them off with his shirt-sleeve. More blood than he'd ever seen before flowed out of the back of Father Santos's head. The man had gashed his head as he fell.

Akira hadn't been sent here to kill someone. Especially not in front of an audience. He gestured to Naoto and the goons.

One of the Filipino women ripped off part of her shirt and used it to stop Father Santos from bleeding. She looked up, but the bousouzoku gang was already gone.

Outside, the thugs from Saitama and Shonan were already speeding away. Akira was the last to get his motorcycle started. Naoto had already left. The best thing he could do would be to get as far away from the crime scene as possible. If the priest died, there would be hell to pay.

But what kind of punishment could Akira expect?

About the author

Shane O'Brien MacDonald was born in 1980 on Cape Breton Island in eastern Canada. He speaks English, Japanese, and Chinese, and has a degree in economics and film studies from Queen's University. Before becoming a novelist he worked as an editor, cinematographer, and assistant picture editor on dozens of films and television shows. He has also been a foreign language instructor at the Tokyo University of Agriculture.

Mr. MacDonald is the author of the Kiki Claymore series of books, which have been described as "post—Ian Fleming female—centric espionage comic books in novel form."